Leo Ware

Claim Ninety-Six

A Border Drama in Five Acts

Leo Ware

Claim Ninety-Six
A Border Drama in Five Acts

ISBN/EAN: 9783337343125

Printed in Europe, USA, Canada, Australia, Japan

Cover: Foto ©Andreas Hilbeck / pixelio.de

More available books at **www.hansebooks.com**

✦Claim Ninety-Six.✦

A BORDER DRAMA

IN FIVE ACTS,

BY

Leo Ware.

———X———

———TO WHICH IS ADDED———

A DESCRIPTION OF THE COSTUMES—CAST OF THE CHARACTERS—
ENTRANCES AND EXITS—RELATIVE POSITIONS OF THE
PERFORMERS ON THE STAGE, AND THE WHOLE
OF THE STAGE BUSINESS.

———X———

———X———

———CLYDE, OHIO:———
AMES' PUBLISHING CO.

CLAIM NINETY-SIX.
CAST OF CHARACTERS.

JERRY MACK	A saloon keeper
GUY LESTER	Mack's partner
CHARLEY GREY	Owner of Claim 96
ARTHUR BRANDON	A banker
MAJOR DOLITTLE	A speculator
PETERSON	A Yankee
SACRAMENTO JOE	A relic of by gone days
EBONY	A colored boot black
NELL, (the Little Nugget)	All pure gold
BELL	Mack's wife
MRS. BRANDON	Brandon's wife
JENNIE LESTER	Guy's sister
BESSIE GREY	Charley's wife
OFFICERS	

SYNOPSIS OF EVENTS.
ACT I.—The Land of Gold.

Scene I—Toomstone, a mining town in California. Jerry Mack's saloon. Guy Lester, king of counterfeitors. Nell. The toast. Claim Ninety-Six. The meanest man. A plan to steal Charley Grey's dust. Arrival of Major Dolittle, from Kentuck. Nell and the Major. A love scene, which ends in "gin and peppermint."

Scene II.—Charley Grey and Mack. Ebony, the boot black. Ebony's advice. Guy Lester, the octoroon. Toomstone quiet. "Slaves, runaway niggers." Ebony keeps his eyes open.

Scene III.—Sacramento Joe and Nell. Nell's history. The little black book. Nell locks Sacramento Joe in the cellar. Bell and Mack. Guy discovers Mack's secret. "Niggor whipper, slave driver." The quarrel. Sacramento Joe. "Don't pull boys, I've got the drop on ye, and I don't give a cuss."

ACT II.—Home of Bell Mack.

Scene I.—Nells advice. Ebony tells Nell of the raid to be made on Charley Grey's cabin. "Nell will be on deck to-night." "I golly, dis chile will be dar' too."

Scene II.—Mack's bad luck. A compact of crime sealed. Nell on the war-path. Ebony's fright. "Now I—I—lay me down."

Scene III.—Charley Grey's cabin. Mack and Guy searching for the gold dust. Timely arrival of Nell and Ebony. "Throw up your hands or you are dead men." Escape of the robbers. Sacramento Joe, "I don't care a cuss."

ACT III.—Arthur Brandon's Home.

Scene I.—The lost child. A living trouble. Bessie Grey deposits the gold dust in Mr. Brandon's safe. Guy Lester interviews Mr. Brandon in regards to the Grey's gold.

Scene II.—Peterson, the apple sass man from Vermont, in search of a meal. Ebony and Peterson. Snubbed by Bessie. "Squashed, tetotally squashed."

Scene III.—Mack and Guy congratulate themselves on their escaping Nell's bullet. "Charley Grey's wife will run Toomstone." Peterson and his four barrels of apple sass. "Polly Ann Spriggins." Peterson proposes to Nell. The game of cards. Bessie Grey interrupts the game. The way to Vermont. The wife beater. Mack faces Nell's rifle the second time.

Scene IV.—Peterson, "a thin pair of pants and a light heart." Murder of Sacramento Joe. Nell on the war-path.

Scene V.—The safe robbery and murder of Mrs. Brandon. Nell arrives on the scene.

ACT IV.—Gold Dust Saloon.

Scene I.—Ebony and Nell. Arrest of Nell for the murder of Mrs. Brandon. "I'm not guilty."

Scene II.—Major Dolittle and Ebony. Jennie, the octoroon, a runaway slave, meets her former master. The slave brand. "I could kill you."

Scene III.—Bell's grief at the arrest of Nell; Ebony's attempt to comfort her. "I golly, dis chile's eyes am leakin'."

ACT V.—Street.

Scene I.—Mack and Guy break open the jail and escape with Nell, the prisoner, to the mountain. Major Dolittle and Ebony arrange a plan to rescue Nell. Guy's secret discovered.

Scene II.—Jennie tells Guy of her meeting Major Dolittle, "that cursed mark." Jennie and Nell in the cave. The quarrel. Jennie's murderous attempt to kill Nell. Mack interferes. The secret of the octoroons disclosed. Jennie stabs Mack. Guy and Jennie escape. Ebony and Major Dolittle rescue Nell. Mack reveals to Nell who her parents are.

Scene III.—Return of Nell, Ebony and Major Dolittle, to Toomstone. News of Mack's death. Charley Grey regains his stolen gold. Nell to return East with her father. Ebony can't be left behind to be hoo-dooed.

STAGE DIRECTIONS.

R., means Right; L., Left; R. H., Right Hand; L. H., Left Hand; C., Centre; 2 E. 2d E.,] Second Entrance; U. E., Upper Entrance; M. D., Middle Door; F., the Flat; D. F., Door in Flat; R. C., Right of Centre; L. C., Left of Centre.

R.	R. C.	C.	L. C.	L.

.*. The reader is supposed to be upon the stage facing the audience.

Claim Ninety-Six.

ACT I.

*SCENE I.—*MACK'*s saloon at Toomstone, California.* Table and chair
R. C.; *bar extending from* C. *to* R.; MACK *leaning on end of bar* C.;
GUY *leaning over bar* R. C., *smoking; as curtain rises* MACK *strikes
bar viciously with open hand.*

Mack. I tell you, old man, if we can do that, and make as good
success of it as we have of the two's and five's, in less than a year our
fortune will run way over the million line, they will be colossial I
tell you, but it is risky, I fear we'll never do it, if we can—

Guy. If we can—bah! I know we can! Didn't I earn the title of
"King of Counterteiters" while I was in the East? Do you think I
have lost any of my skill since coming out here? No sir! I can
engrave as good a plate to-day as I could ten years ago; you haven't
heard any complaint from the two's and five's yet, have you?

Mack. Thunder! no, they won'd pass with the cashier of any bank.

Guy. And if I don't engrave plates for ten's and twenty's that
will do the same, I'l—I'll—well I'll agree to drink all the old rotten
shotgun whi-key you've got in this—this—(*looks around*) this place
of yours, Mack. (*laughing*) There! you couldn't ask a man to do
anything more desp rate than that, could you?

Mack. (*goes behind bar*) There old man, that's all right—(*sets out
bottle*) let's imbibe, that's reliable: the common run of cow-boy's
don't get to see that bottle—take something.

Guy. No! a man in the busine-s I am, needs a clear and level
head, an I he can't have that and drink your whiskey, Mack; but
about the plates for the twenty's—you have never seen any of Jennie's
work, have you? Well here. (*takes out bill and throws it on bar*) look
at that. (MACK *examines bill closely*) Well, what do you think of
that, pretty good, eh? Think th t would pass?

Mack. Thunder! yes, I would take it my-elf, if you hadn't said it
was queer. You don't mean to say that your s'ster engraved that
plate, do you?

Guy. That's exactly what I do say; she not only engraved it, but
she printed it too.

Mack. The devil! (*examines bill*) Say, old man, is the whole
family counterfeiters? If they are, your father must have been
some thing extraordinary. Say, where did he work?

Guy. That's none of your darned business, Mr. Jerry Mack. I've
told you several times that you didn't need to know anything about
my antecedents. Our business relation is just this and no more—I

print the money and you pass it off, that is just as far as we go, do you understand?

Mack. Oh! That's all right, here take something an I we won't say anything more about it, the twenty's will be a success, I am sure of that.

Guy. Well then, just once, *(raises bottle)* here's success to the ten's and twenty's, and hoping that we will make a million.

Enter, NELL, L., 1 E.

Nell. Hold on there, Guy, I want to join you in that. (NELL *goes behind counter, takes glass*) Now then, here, let me add a little to that toast—here's hoping that we all will make a million a piece and I shall gain a husband before the year is out. (*touch glasses and drink*) Well!

Mack. Well, what?

Nell. Well, that's the best speculation that's been made in Toom-stone since I've known anything about the camp.

Mack. Speculation?

Nell. Yes, spec—u—lation, that's what I said.

Guy. Whos' been making a speculation? Tell us all about it, Nell.

Nell. (*to* MACK) How much did you sell "Claim 96" for?

Mack. That was about the best speculation that's been made for some time. I got $500 out of old "96."

Nell. And you thought it wasn't worth fifty cents.

Mack. Thought? I know it. I wouldn't give Guy twenty-five cents for it to-day. Guy can tell you the worth of "96."

Nell. Just the same, Charley Grey has struck it rich!

Mack. What?

Guy. Ah! a pocket, Nell, it won't pan out anything.

Nel. No sir! A strong, heavy vein, I tell you, free from quartz, and the assayer says it will go to seventy per cent, and maybe eighty.

Mack. What a fool I was for ever selling old "96," Guy. (*to* NELL) Who told you about it, Nell?

Nell. Nobody! I seen it with my own eyes. I went with Charley down to the assayers office; you ought to have seen that old clerk's eyes bulge out when Charley showed him a pan full of the dirt. Say, Guy, I'll shake you the box for the drinks. (*picks up dice box*)

Guy. What's he going to do with his claim?

Nell. Charley says he is going to work old "96" for all she is worth. Old Brandon, the banker, offered him fifty thousand for the mine, but Charley refused, and then Brandon offered him thirty thousand for a half interest.

Mack. Thunderation!

Nell. Lord! You ought to see Charley's cabin, he's got gold piled up on the floor a foot deep.

Guy. Nell, you are giving us a breeze now. Has Grey really struck it rich at last?

Nell. You bet he has! He has got lots of gold down in his cabin, not a foot deep, though. Mack, you old schemer, that's one of your speculations that didn't pan out well. (*starts R.*)

Mack. Hold on! Where are you going?

Nell. Charley bet me an ounce of dust a while ago, that he could

beat me shooting with a rifle, and I just want to show him that he
can't shoot a little bit. (*exit, R.,* 1 E.

Mack. Well, don't be gone long. I want you to 'tend bar awhile.
I am going down to see Grey. (*t, GRY*) Old man, let's sit down,
that news has made me shakey: (*seated R. C.*) and that fool of a
tenderfoot Grey has struck it rich at last.

Guy. (*seated R. C.*) Seems that way.

Mack. Guy, we've been partners for about a year in the green
goods business, havn't we?

Guy. About a year I think, an l in that year you have tried, at
least seven hundred different schemes to chisel me out of money,
havn't you Mack? You are the most miserly man I ever done business with. Honestly Mack, you are the meanest man I ever saw,
you'd pasture a goat on your mother's grave.

Mack. (*laughing*) Oh! well, if a fellow don't look out for himself
these days, who will look out for him? I am in the West for what
money there is in it, and not for my health. But about this partner-
ship business—how would you like to go in deeper—that is, if there
is any money in it, and I think there is.

Guy. Well, I don't know, explain yourself, Mack.

Mack. Well, Charley Grey has struck it rich.

Guy. Yes, that's a dead sure thing, Charley Grey has struck it
rich—Well!

Mack. And he keeps his gold in his cabin.

Guy. Not so sure of that Mack—Well!

Mack. O! drop that infernal *well* of yours, Guy, it grows
monotonous. Listen—suppose you and I go down to Grey's cabin
to-night, while he is away, and take what gold he has. I know
where he keeps it, we can get it and no one be the wiser, and then
we can get him in here—get him to drink some—

Guy. Yes, if we get him to drink any of this "stomach corosive"
you keep, Mack, you can get him to do anything.

Mack. We'll get him to drink and then get him in a game of cards
and cheat him out of what gold he has left.

Guy. Well, of all the low down, mean, two faced, thieving, cool-
headed rascally men I ever knew, you take the banner, Mack, you
take the whole culinary department for cussedness.

Mack. Don't get so personal, Guy; what do you say? Will you
help?

Guy. Well, I never done any of that kind of work before—but
here's my hand on it, and you may rely on me. (*they shake hands*

Maj. (*out L.*) Hello! there, I say; house! house! Landlord! bar-
tender! anybody! send a nigger out here, or come out yourself and
take my horse—Gad, do you want a fellah to starve? Hello! house!
house!

Guy. What the deuce is that? (*looks L.*) Ho! Mack, another
innocent for you to fleece, and I'll wager that you'll do it too!

Mck. (*goes L., 1 E.*) Hitch yer horse and come in stranger.
(*to GY*) Thunderation! Guy, here come's Stonewall Jackson.

Guy. Well, I'll see you again in an hour or so. (*exit, R.,* 1 E.

Mack. All right! (*goes L., 1 E.*) Come in stranger, come in
don't stand on ceremony here, come in.

Enter, MAJOR DOLITTLE, L., 1 E.

Maj. Begad! sah, I can't say that I like your hospitality—(*hold
ing nose*) Faugh! is this a saloon or a glue factory?

Mack. Thunder! what do you mean? This is a saloon, of course.
What did you take it for? A tan yard?

Maj. You better go and—whew—(*whistles*) where does that diabolical odor come from?

Mack. O! that's limberger cheese. (*retires behind bar*

Maj. Well, begad sah, you'd better lead it out. (*goes L. C.*)
Give me some gin and peppermint. I suppose you could furnish—
(*stops and stares at* MACK) well, by gad!

Mack. Well, what in thunder is the matter with you? Didn't
you ever see a stranger before?

Maj. Well, begad sah, I never saw a stranger before that looks
so much like my old slave driver, John Sands.

Mack. (*goes L. C., startled—aside*) Thunderation?

Maj. I suppose sah, that you don't know John Sands?

Mack. No! sir, no! sir, never heard tell of him before, or you
either.

Maj. Well, that's all right then; give me some gin and peppermint. (MACK *serves him*) This is a pretty common saloon, ain't it?
Begad sah, I'm used to drinking before a looking-glass.

Mack. Then you haven't been in the West very long. I might
put in a fine mirror and a seventy-five dollar pyramid, and the first
cow-boy that come in drunk, would see how many pieces he could
shoot them into.

Maj. Then sah, be gad, I'd shoot him. (*flourishes revolver*

Mack. The boys out here want whiskey, and they would rather
drink it out of tin cups than cut glass.

Maj. By gad, sah, I'm glad I stopped here. Give me some diabolical gin and peppermint. I want to stop here with you a few days
—I'm Major Dolittle, from Kentuckey, be gad sah.

Mack. (*excited, goes L. C.—aside*) Thunder! my old employer;
what ill luck has brought him here?

Maj. Be gad, sah, I used to own a hundred niggers before the war;
when the cussed abolitionists came down and freed 'em. I used to
have a fellah hired to whip niggers and do other chores for me—his
name was John Sands—he stole a hundred dollars from me, be gad,
and cut sticks for the West; you look enough like John Sands to be
his twin brother, be gad sah; if I ever find that man, I'll put a hole
through his diabolical heart, that you can throw a Chinese bible
through, and I more than half way believe you are the man.

(*flourishes revolver*

Mack. But I tell you I am not! I was born and raised here in
this section of the country; and I'll tell you another thing too, I
don't allow every stranger that comes along, to give me the lie; now
sir, let's drop the subject.

Maj. All right sah, if you ain't John Sands, why—why be gad,
sah, give me some gin and peppermint. I came to this country to
invest in mining lands, and be gad, sah, I've got the money to pay
for 'em too. I want the best room you've got in your diabolical
house, sah, and here's ten dollars to pay for it, give me your register and I'd sign my name. I'm Major Dolittle, from Kentucky, sah.
I used to own one hundred niggers, two moon-shine distillerys, and
the biggest tobacco plantation in the State; (MACK *throws out register*) I always sign my name with an X.

Mack. Here! let me write your name for you.

Maj. If you don't like the way I write my name, sah, maybe, you will meet me in a little affair of honah in the morning, be gad, sah, and I choose pistols for the weapons.

Mack. No sir! I decline to fight you.

Maj. Then sah, if you won't fight, I'll take some gin and peppermint.

Mack. (*goes* R., 1 E., *calls*) Nell! O! Nell! come here and watch the bar, I'm going down to see Grey.

Enter, NELL, R., 1 E.

Nell. All right governor! here I am and you can bet your last nugget on me, I'll keep things straight.

(*goes behind bar and works vigorously*)

Mack. I'll not be gone long, Nell, half an hour, maybe.

(*exit,* L., 1 E.

Nell. Stay all day if you want too.

Maj. (R. C.—*aside*) Be gad, Major, that's a diabolical good looking girl. (NELL *brushing clothes, etc.*) It's been some time since you've had a chance to look at a pretty girl, sah, but I flatter myself, you've got a good appearance; now for a little love making. What's the matter with that diabolical heart of mine? Be gad, it's right up in my mouth. Now Major, play your cards to your own advantage, and use your infatuating powers the best you know how. Ahem! (*aloud*) I'm Major Dolittle, from Kentucky, sah, and—and—and be gad sah, I'll take some gin an l peppermint.

SCENE II.—Street.

Enter, MACK, L., 1 E., CHARLEY GREY, R., 1 E., *they meet* C.

Mack. Hello! Charley, how are you? I had just started down to see you. They tell me that you've struck it rich at last. I want to congratulate you on your good luck.   (*shake hands*

Charley. Yes, Mack, after so long a time I have struck "pay dirt." I am afraid that the selling of old "96" was a bad speculation for you, Mack.

Mack. Ah! that's all right Charley, of course I didn't get the real worth of the mine, but I like to help a fellow along when he needs it. When I sold you "Claim 96" you had been here in Toomstone for a year, and hadn't made a dollar, while I had been here about two years and made plenty of money. My motto is "Live and let live."

Chas. And that's a good motto for any man to have. Mack, you have been a royal good friend to me, and Charley Grey ain't the man to go back on his friends.

Ebony. (*out* R., *sings*) 'O! I carry my shop upon my back."

Enter, EBONY, R. E.

Hello! dar Charley, lemme shine yer boots, only five cents.

Mack. Hello! there Ebony, I thought you had left these diggings.

Ebony. Hi golly! no boss, I'se here fo' de reason, I tells yo'. Hi dar boss Charley, you done been gone and struck it rich at last, ain' yo'? Lemme shine yer shoes fer you.

Chas. Yes, go ahead, give them a good shine, now mind you, Ebony.

Mack. Well, Charley, come down to the "Gold Dust bar" to-night and we will get up a nice little game. Lester and one or two others will be down there. *(starts, R.*

Ebony. Hi golly! Charley, didn't I done go fer to tell yer dat yer goin' ter make a fortune yet? *(shining* CHARLEY'S *shoes*

Chas. All right, Mack! I'll be down to-night. *(to* EBONY*)* Yes, Ebony, I've struck a good vein, and if it holds out I am on the high road to fortune.

Mack. *(aside)* And on the high road to the devil too, if I don't fleece you, I miss my guess, that's all. *(exit, R., 1 E.*

Ebony. I tell you boss, we'se all goin' to strike it rich some time sho', if we jist got de stayin' quality, jist sho' to. I golly, when I first came here to dis place, I us'ter think dat I'd never get 'nuff money ahead to buy me a looking-glass to see myself starve to death, but I tell you boss, I'm way out of sight now, but if I was you Charley, I wouldn't trust dat feller, Mack.

Chas. Why not, Ebony? Don't you think he is honest?

Ebony. Tell you boss, he talks too smooth; I be ieve he'd steal.

Chas. But he has always been a friend of mine. He sold me "Claim 96" for a great deal less than he gave for it.

Ebony. And when he sold you dat claim he didn't think it was worth anything. You better take a niggers advice. I tell you he'll steal, and dat feller comin' down de street yonder, *(points* L., 1 E.*)* better watch him too.

Chas. *(looks* L., 1 E.*)* Oh! Guy Lester, I don't like him very well. He always wears good clothes and has plenty of money.

Ebony. And, I golly, he never works none, either; nobody knows anything about him or Mack either, nobody knows where dey come from. I tell you boss, dey'll steal.

Chas. Well, there may be something in what you say, Ebony, and it won't do any harm to watch them a little. I don't feel in the mood to talk to Lester now, so I'll just walk down the street. *(exit, R., 1 E.*

Ebony. *(looking* R., 1 E.*)* I gol'y, white man's mighty curo's, I bet he makes a fool out'en himself; most white folks do when dey find something dey ain't expectin'. I golly, he never paid me for shinin' dem shoes. *(calls)* Hi dar! boss Charley! golly wait. *(rushes out* R., 1 E.*

Enter, GUY LESTER, L., 1 E.

Guy. Cuss the niggers, it always gives me the shivers to see one. I wonder if I ever can overcome my hatred of the race? Not likely, when I take the second thought and know that some of the same blood courses through my veins, and that I have been a slave, that I have had to acknowledge myself another man's property, to do his bidding, to work with the other niggers, as he has often expressed it; or take the lash at the hands of an over-bearing slave driver—a "nigger-whipper"—who would count it a crime for running away from such a man as that? Bah! I wish I could exterminate the whole accursed race, at once.

Enter, JENNIE LESTER, R., 1 E.

Jennie. Hello! Guy, what are you doing here?
Guy. What! Jennie? What are you here for?

Jen. Well, I heard that the Regulators of Toomstone were about waking up again, so I came down to see if I could learn anything about it.

Guy. O! the Regulators are all right, they will never do anything, they can't afford to track thieves, there's too many thieves among themselves.

Jen. How does it come that you are here in Toomstone? Thought you were up on the "Divide."

Guy. O! Mack and I were arranging some business for to-night.

Jen. And what were you standing out here on the street by yourself for? Oh! I know, you were brooding over that old trouble: will you never forget?

Guy. Forget? How can a man forget when he has to wear that accursed mark to the grave: (*holds out hand with S marked on back*) and you too, Jennie, (*takes JENNIE'S hand, S on back*) how can you ask me to forget and these marks stareing me in the face?

Jen. But we are free, now Guy, to do as we please, we are not the property of any man now. We are free, I say, and let any man deny it if he dares—(*draws small dirk*) but we are the only ones here that know of our past life.

Guy. Bah! but the dread, the suspense—sometimes we may see someone who will recognize us as slaves, runaway niggers; someone may find out our past life—then what? I tell you girl, the thought is almost maddening.

Jen. Let them find out, but let anyone breathe one word and— (*raises dirk*) but don't speak of slaves, runaway niggers; for heaven's sake! don't mention that, Guy. We have seen trouble enough while we were in bondage; don't speak of it now, when we are far away from it. There is no danger of anyone finding us out, we have changed our name—

Guy. That amounts to nothing—what's in a name? There is the trouble. (*shows hand*) I tell you—sometimes that cursed mark burns and sears the flesh like a coal of fire. There would be more honor in being as black as midnight—then you are not in dread, you are known. Sometimes I think I could cut that hand off, throw it in the fire and watch it burn—anything to destroy, and be rid of that mark.

Jen. O! Guy! Guy! don't get yourself in such a fearful rage, come, go home with me and we will go to work and forget all about that hateful mark. Come—

Guy. No! I shall stay here—you go, and you may go to work on the plates for the ten's and twenty's. Mack will be up to see them sometime to-morrow. I shall be home sometime to-night or in the morning—you are not afraid?

Jen. Afraid?   (*shows dirk, exit, L., 1 E.*)

Guy. (*looking L., 1 E.*) Few men have such a faithful sister as I have. Ah! if it wasn't for that blight (*raises hand*) I could be somebody yet. Why did my life have to be so cursed? An octoroon— an eighth blood—(*draws revolver*) I've a good mind to put an end to my existence, but no! I have an abhorence—a hatred against the world. I'll live, and any crime, any action I can do against mankind, I'll do it. For men have made me what I am, and now they must look out, I am desperate.

Enter, MACK, R., 1 E., *slaps* GUY *on shoulder.*

Mack. Well Guy!

Guy. O! Mack, you are back, are you?

Mack. Yes, and everything is coming our way. I tell you I have found out everything about Grey, we need to know. He keeps his gold hid in one corner of his cabin. The lock on the door is a very clumsy affair, a small piece of wire will remedy that. Thunderation! Guy, it is the most inviting job I ever saw.

Guy. Mack, you are taking this very cool, it strikes me that you must be an old hand at the business.

Mack. You told me awhile ago that I need not know anything about your ancestors; now I'll tell you that you don't need to know anything about my past.

Guy. Well, I guess we are about even on that score, Mack: but look here, suppose Grey comes back to his cabin and finds us there, then what?

Mack. And suppose he don't do anything of the kind? Thunderation! isn't the chances as good one way as the other? I think they are better, if he does come in and finds us in his cabin, we can frame up some kind of a lie, and if he don't come, then we will be a couple of thousands ahead.

Guy. Mack, do you expect Grey to stay away of his own accord?

Mack. No! I've been talking to him until he thinks I am the best friend he has. I must go down to the "Gold Dust," Grey said he would be down there, and we can't afford to let the friendship between us grow cold now. *(starts* L.) O! by the way, *(turning)* I thought of another plan awhile ago. Grey carries his claim papers with him all the time, so we can get him drunk and steal his papers from him, and we will be the owners of old "96," and then if he makes a fuss about it, we can say that he sold the claim to us. We can write out a receipt you know—that's a good plan, don't you think so? Well, I must be going. You come down to the "Gold Dust" after awhile and we will finish our arrangements for that little affair of to-night. *(exit,* L.)

Guy. *(looking* L.) Of all the rascally, scoundrels in existence you must be the worst, Jerry Mack. (EBONY *looks in* R.) I fear you more than any other living man: if you knew my secret, it would be noised from the Mississippi river to the Pacific coast. If I could only learn the secret of your past, then we would be even. You have a secret, I am sure, and I shall make it my business to find out what that secret is. *(exit,* L., 1 E.

Enter, EBONY, R., 1 E., *slips after* GUY.

Ebony. And I'll show you dat a fool nigger's got some sense. If I don't keep de white of my eye over in your direction. I hope I may chew all of de bristles outn't my shoe brush. *(exit,* L., 1 E.

SCENE III.—MACK's *saloon;* SACRAMENTO JOE *seated* R. C., NELL *seated on box* L. *of* JOE.

Joe. Them's my sentiments exactly, precisely, just to a dot, and I don't give a cuss. It's a shame, Nell, a burnin' shame fer him ter keep you here in Toom-tone, in this here hole of pure cussedness, ter make you stay here and serve out his slop over that bar to these here miners, what ain't any better nor a dumb brute—a animal what walks on four feet. You orter be some'rs in the East, in school or—or—somethin'—

Nell. Why Joe! he says I know too much now.

Joe. Yes, that's jist like his "dod burne l" chinnin' to talk that'er way. I say you orter be in school, an l I'm goin' ter tell him so, too. Them's my sentiments and I don't give a cuss.

Nell. He wouldn't let me go, Joe, 'cause he says, he's my—my—what do you call it?

Joe. Yer—yer gardeen. Nell, that's it persactly and that's another one of his "dod burned" lies too. Mack's alers been a rascal and he alers will be. Them's my sentiments jist to a dot and I don't give a cuss. I've knowed him fer a—   *(stops suddenly)*

Nell. Well, what made you stop, Joe? You tol l me once that you had only been in this part of California for two years, and of course you didn't know Mack before then.

Joe. O! incourse, incourse, I'de never seed him afore then, but don't you pay too perticlar 'tention to what I was 'er sayin', gal. I said that Jerry Mack was 'er rascal, and dot burn him he is too. He ain't no more yer gardeen nor I am. Them's my sentiments persactly and I don't give a cuss. How di l he git you anyway?

Nell. Why, he said in 1850, there was a wagon train passed through Nevada, close to where he was working in a silver mine—the next morning he was out on the prairie looking for some stray horses and he found me, and that I had got lost from the wagon train. I was about two years old then, an l when Mack took me to the camp the miners said they would call me Nugget Nell, and that's been my name ever since.

Joe. Persactly, and Mack said that was in 1850; now let me figer a little—this is 1865, and fifty and ten is sixty, and five is sixty-five, that makes fifteen years and you was two years old when he found you, that makes two more, consequently you are seventeen years old.

Nell. But I am older than that, Joe. I am nineteen, I found that wrote down in a little book that Mack keeps hid.

Joe. Then them dates is another one of his dod burne l mistakes, 'cause figers won't lie. I tell you Nell, Mack's a rascal. Them's my sentiments jist to a dot and I don't give a cuss. He knows who you belong to jist as well as—as—as any other man. I wish I had that ttle book that you say he keeps hi l.

Nell. Well, I can get it for you Joe, if you'll never tell.

Joe. Well, I'll never tell.

Nell. Honest?

Joe. Honest! "honor bright."

Nell. Hope to fall down a raft and break your neck, if you do?

Joe. Break my neck if I do. Them's my sentiments.

Nell. Well then, I'll watch and the first chance I have, I'll pick the lock of his desk and steal it.

Joe. Nell, if you'll do that, the first nugget I find I'll give to you, I don't care if it's as big as a house.

Nell. All right! I'll get the book for you, you can rely on me, I ain't no marked deck. I'm straight and you can bet your last scale of dust on that, Joe.

Joe. Them's the sentiments, Nell, persactly. You git me that

book and I'll bet my claim—what ain't nothin' but imagination—that
we will have you in school in the East in less than two months.

Nell. I don't believe I'd like to go there. I'll rather stay here.

Joe. Now look here, you jist rely on Sacramenter Joe, fer I tell
you, when you git to the East you'll like it so well, you'll never want
to come back here. Them's my sentiments.

Nell. I'd want to come back and see you sometimes, Joe.

Joe. No! you wouldn't, you'd soon forget old Joe. Why do I
turn it gal, you don't know how much difference there is between
the East and this place; why you'd be dressed in silk—

Nell. Is silk nicer than old faded blue calico?

Joe. (*laughs*) Ha! ha! ha! O! listen at her, "Is silk nicer than
calico?" Well I think it is Nell, a dod burned right nicer. Silk
shines so you can see yourself in it, and then you'd have a nice straw
hat with green ribbon on it and a little red umbreller fer to keep off
the sun.

Nell. The sun can't hurt me Joe, I'm used to it.

Joe. Well, you'd need a red umbreller when you go East.

Nell. (*laughs*) Ha! ha! ha! if I was to dress up that way,
wouldn't I cut a figure, Joe? Ha! ha! ha!

Joe. You'd soon get used to it—jist think of the nice things you'd
see, b'g fine buildin's and—

Nell. Why, don't you think this country is nice, Joe? The trees,
and mountains, and rocks and the mines, why I think they are just
grand.

Joe. Yes, but not like the East.

Nell. Is there really so much difference between the West and
East?

Joe. You bet! Why dod burn it gal, I'd bet my last nugget on
that every time. Them's my sentiments persactly, and I don't care
a cuss.

Nell. Don't the girls there have to 'tend old dirty bars like I do
here in the "Gold Dust?"

Joe. No sir! The girls there ride in their carriages and have a
nigger to drive their horses for em'. (NELL *drops her head in her
hands and study's deeply*) and then you git good grub out thare, old
fashioned pumpkin pie and sich like. I tell you Nell, I'd go furder
right now fer a piece of real old fashioned, New England Pumpkin
pie, than anything else on earth; dod burned ef I wouldn't. Now
them's my sentiments persactly, and I don't give a cuss.

Enter, CHARLEY, L., 2 E.

Hello! Charley, struck it rich, haven't you? Come here and let me
shake yer hand.   (*they shake hands*

Chas. Yes, struck it rich at last, Joe, and my days of poverty are
at an end. Ah! Joe, many's the time that I've gone to bed hungry,
and wondering where my breakfast was to come from, but those
days are past, for if "Claim 96" holds out like she opens up, I'm Jay
Gould, Joe.

Joe. Persactly, them's the sentiments.

Chas. But what's the matter here? (*points to* NELL) She seems
unusually quiet; not sick are you Nell?

Joe. No! she's not sick, she's studyin'. I've been givin' her a lecture about the East, and she can't hardly take it all in, she kinder thinks Joe's a lyin' to her.

Nell. No! I don't Joe, I know you wouldn't lie to me, but it all seems so strange. (*to* CHARLEY) Is there really so much difference between the East and the West, Charley?

Chas. Yes, Nell, there is a vast difference, you can rely on all that Joe tells you.

Joe. Persactly, them's the sentiments, thank ye Charley.

Chas. Well, I must be moving, or I shall be overtaken by darkness—

Nell. Are you going away, Charley?

Chas. O! only over on the "Divide." I hear that there is a fellow over there—Major Dolittle, I believe his name is—wants to invest in mining stock, and I thought I might dispose of part of my claim to him; and Nell, I sent for my wife several days ago, she may come on this evening's stage, and if she does, you take care of her until I come back in the morning.

Nell. All right! Charley, you can bank on me every time, you bet on that. (*exit*, CHARLEY, L., 2 E.

Joe. Them's the sentiments, persactly jist to a dot, N H, and I don't give a cuss, and there will be another chance fer you to find out more about the East, ef that gal comes here and I 'spose she will. Why dod burn it, Nell, ef you was in the East, you'd git a husband in less than a year.

Nell. But I don't want a husband. I'd rather have a friend that I could come and talk to like you, Joe. When a fellow gets married they have to quarrel like Mack and his wife; they quarrel all the time, and of course everybody else is the same.

Joe. Not much they ain't. No sir! not by a dod burned sight. Nell, say you go bring old Joe a chew of dog leg terbacker. I've sot here and chinned so long to you and Charley, that my mouth's as dry as a brick yard.

Nell. Let's get up some excitement over it, Joe. I'll pitch coppers with you to see whether I get it for you, or you get it yourself.

Joe. Them's the sentiments, gal, have you got a dod burned copper? Old Joe's broke, persactly.

Nell. I've got the coppers, now then, head or tails?

Joe. Heads, them's my sentiments.

Nell. (*tosses up penny, they both cry out, as penny strikes the floor*) You've lost. There Joe, it's rolled down in the cellar.

Joe. I'll go and get the dod burned thing.

(*raises trap-door* R. C. *and goes down*

Nell. (*closes trap-door—laughs*) Ha! ha! ha! Joe, you are my prisoner and I'm going to keep you, too.

Joe. (*under stage*) Gal, you open that dod burned trap-door and let me out.

Nell. No sir! no sir! no sir! *dances off* R., 2 E., *singing*) No sir! no sir! etc.

Enter, MACK and GUY, L., 2 E., *they lean over bar.*

Mack. And that was another good scheme, Guy, getting Grey to go over on the "Divide" to-night. He will be completely out of our way; we have nothing to fear.

Guy. That is, from Grey, but that nigger, Ebony, has been following me around all day, he may have over-heard some of our con-

versation, and he never had any time for me or you either, Mack.
He may drop in on us or tell someone else.

Mack. What? Two of us and afraid of that boy? Thunderation!
no, he won't do anything, but let him show himself around here
and I'll soon fix him.

Enter, BELL, R., 2 E.

Bell. Jerry—
Mack. What? Eavesdropping again. (*jerks her* C.) How long
have you been standing there? Don't study up some lie now, tell
me the truth.
Bell. I haven't been eavesdropping. I just come to—
Mack. Shut up! didn't I tell you once that I didn't propose to
have my movements spyed upon? I meant every word I said. You
try this sneaking game on me once more and I'll find a way to cure
you of it, that you'll remember.
Bell. But I wasn't spying on you, I came to tell you—
Mack. Didn't I say that I didn't want to hear any of your lies?
Guy. Let her tell what she came for. Mack.
Mack. Well then, out with it, but no lies, mind. When I say any
thing I mean it; now let's have your story.
Bell. I have no story to tell—
Mack. Just as I thought, Guy, she's—
Bell. I came to tell you that Charley Grey's wife came on the
stage a few minutes ago, and she wants to know where he is.
Mack. Thunderation! Guy, that will—(*checks himself suddenly*)
you tell her that Charley's over on the "Divide" and won't be back
till morning; you keep her here till Charley comes back. Now go—
you are not wanted here, do you understand?
Bell. (*turning*) You may see the time Jerry, when you'll want
me—
Mack. Shut up and get out here, or (*raises hand*) I'll spoil your
beauty. (*exit,* BELL, R.
Guy. Mack, if Charley's wife has come, we will have to drop our
little excursion to-night.
Mack. No! we will finish our arrangements right now and be o'T.
I'll watch outside the cabin and you can go in and get the gold.
Guy. You'll do nothing of the kind, Mr. Jerry Mack, we will both
go in after the gold.
Mack. Well then, if I do that and there is two thousand, I'll take
twelve hundred—
Guy. I differ from you there, too, we will share equally or not at
all. Understand that?
Mack. Didn't I find out about the gold and didn't I lay all of the
plans? I say I'll have twelve hundred of it.
Guy. And I say you'll not, Mr. John Sands.
Mack. (*started*) Thunderation! what do you mean?

(*hand to pocket*
Guy. (*presents revolver*) Just what I say! Take that hand away
from your pocket, or you are a dead man. Mack, you dropped a
paper out on the street and I found it. Listen and I will read it to
you: (*reads*) "Louisville, K'y., Aug. 27, 1858, I, John Sands, do
hereby agree to work for Major Frank Dolittle, in the capacity of
over-seer of slaves in the tobacco fields during the summer seasons.

and in the tobacco sheds during the winter seasons, for which services I am to receive the sum of $50 per month—payable monthly. Signed John Sands." There Mr. John Sands, alias Jerry Mack, what do you say to that?

Mack. It's a lie, an infernal lie.

Guy. Listen to what is written on the back: (*reads*) "Nov. 16, 1858, I have this day stolen two hundred dollars from Dolittle; think we are even now." That's another lie is it? Thief, slave driver, nigger whipper. (L. C.

Mack. Curse you Guy Lester! (*tries to draw revolver*

(JOE *pushes up trap-door and springs on stage, presents two pistols.*

Joe. Don't pull boys, fer I've got the drop on ye—persactly. Them's my sentiments and I don't give a cuss.

PICTURE—SLOW CURTAIN.

END OF ACT I.

ACT II.

SCENE I.—Interior of MACK's *house.* BELL *and* NELL *seated* L. C.,

Bell. Nell, I don't see how I am to stand this any longer, this life is worse than a prison. He threatened to strike me to-day. I don't know what to do or which way to turn.

Nell. I know what I'd do, I'd scratch his eyes out, if I was in your place. I'd leave him, that's what I'd do and you can bet your dust on that.

Bell. If I was to leave, he would follow me and bring me back, then my life would be ten times worse than it is now. No! that would never do, Nell.

Nell. Then I'd get a pick handle and smash that cast iron skull of his. There, how does that "pointer" suit you?

Bell. O! Nell! Nell!

Nell. Well then, if you don't like that, here's another way; shake him the box for the drinks and put some arsenic in his—

Bell. Why Nell! you wouldn't kill him, would you?

Nell. You just bet I would or any other man, if he treated me like Jerry Mack treats you, of course I'd kill him. Why not?

Bell. O! Nell! Nell, this wild, rough life is ruining you the same as it is me. If we could only go away from it all, far away, where we would never see or hear anything that would make me think of my unhappy past, where you could be in school, and away from this evil influence and associates. If we could only be where there is culture and refinement. O! Nell, this life is killing me; we shall yet see a tragic ending, for I am sure that Jerry is not getting all of his money honestly. What if he is a highway-man, and if he is found out: think of the disgrace, Nell.

Ebony. (*out* L., *sings*) "I carry my shop upon my back."

EBONY *rushes in* L., 1 E.

Say dar Nell, kin you tell—(*sees* BELL) I golly, you looks white as chalk, what's de matter—sick?

Bell. No! Ebony, I'm not sick, I have a headache, that's all.

(*exit, R., 2 F.*

Ebony. (*looking R., 2 F.*) I-gol-ly ef dat 'oman ain't sick, den I hope I'll never shine another shoe. (*to NELL*) Say, kin you done tole me where boss Charley am?

Nell. Why, he's gone over on the "Divide;" what do you want with him?

Ebony. 'Pears to me you'se mi'ty 'quisitive, but I'll done tell yer, 'cause your a friend of mine. Dat ar' snake, dat ar' dumed copper head, dat ar' rattle snake—

Nell. Oh! wind up and start over, niggers can't talk no how. What are you trying to say?

Ebony. Why, I was goin' down de street awhile ago and I seed dat ar' dumed, onery, prairie dog, water mocasin. I golly!

Nell. Well, why don't you say it?

Ebony. Dat ar' dumed sneak Guy Lester agoin' down de street and a talkin' to hisself, likes if he was interested—

Nell. Well, he's got a right to talk to himself if he wants too. Let him talk, tain't none of your business, you haven't any right to stop him.

Ebony. But—but— but golly Nell, he said as how, if Charley was gone he'd—he'd—fo' de good Lord sake, Nell, if boss Charley's gone, he's goin' to steal all his dust to-night.

Nell. What! are you sure? (*grabs EBONY and shakes him*

Ebony. Well, do you think I'd lie 'bout it? (*crying*) Dat's—too—much—to—think—dat—m—my—best friend—'ud think—I'd—I'd—I—I—lie—bobo—'bout dat. (*coat sleeve act*

Nell. Well, you can bet all of your dust on one thing, Nell will be on deck to-night.

Ebony. (*brightening up*) I'll bet all de bristles out'en my shine brush, I'll be dar too, and I'll be armed to de teeth too, I golly.

(*exit, L., 1 E.*

Enter, BELL, R., 2 E.

Bell. Has Ebony gone, Nell? What did he want? O! he gave me such a shock, I was almost sure he had come to tell me something about Jerry—

Enter, MACK, L., 2 E.

Mack. Seems to me you are putting yourself to a great deal of trouble on my account—I'll tell you one thing, Jerry is able to take care of hi'nself—now get out of here, I want to use this room awhile.

Bell. Has it come to this, that you order me from my own room, after all that—

Mack. What! not gone yet? Get out of here—go to the kitchen where you belong. Don't stand there staring at me like a big wax doll—go! or I'll— (*raises hand*

Nell. Jerry Mack, you strike her and I'll save the Regulators a job. Do you understand that? (*exit, BELL, R., 2 E., slowly*

Mack. You and Bell have got a fit of the sulks. I am able to run my own house yet awhile; now get out of here, I want this room— get I say.

Nell. Jerry Mack, you go to thunder, I am not your wife. (*MACK sneaks out* L., 2 E.) you can't order me around you old buzzard, you can bet your dust on that.

EBONY *sneaks in from* R., 2 E.

Ebony. (C.) I golly.

SCENE II.—*Street scene. Lights down.*

Mack. (C.) Thunderation! I'd rather stand up to a square shouldered fight any time than be whipped by a woman's tongue. Cuss 'em, Bell has got a fit of the sulks and Nell is full of her high-toned notions. Somebody is meddling with my affairs, and I believe it's Sacramento Joe; the old fool will set and talk all day. If I find out that it is him, I'll learn him a lesson that he won't forget in a hurry. I'd give something to know who he is and where he came from, but he is as close as an oyster, when it comes to talking about himself. Luck is running against me lately, but it may come my way again. Thunder! what a foolish trick it was in me, pulling those papers out of my pocket on the street; the way my luck has been lately, I might have known that I would lose something, or— well there's no use in crying over spilled milk; I dropped the paper and Lester found it, and now I am in his power and I suppose he will—

Enter, GUY, R., 1 E.

Guy. Use that power? You just bet your life I will, Mr. "nig-ger-whipper" John Sands.

Mack. Lester, don't kick a man when he is down. You have learned my secret and you can send me back East and have me im-prisoned if you want to, I am at your mercy, but as far as me being a "nigger-whipper" you needn't throw that in my teeth. I worked —or whipped slaves—for so much money—

Guy. And if you didn't have money enough, you stole what you thought you needed. Is that what you mean?

Mack. Being a slave driver is nothing dishonorable, or wasn't be-fore slavery was abolished—but counterfeiting—

Guy. Is about as dishonorable as going to a miner's cabin and stealing his dust. Eh! Mack?

Mack. Suppose the government finds out we are in the green goods business, who will serve the longest term, you or I?

Guy. Look here Mack, just because I happened to find out a secret of your past life, it's no reason we should not still be friends; we can't afford to be enemies, here's my hand, I am willing to be just as we have been in the past. Come, what do you say?

Mack. We will be friends, Guy.   (*they shake hands*

Guy. Oh! glad to hear you say that. I don't like to make enemies, Mack. I have too many of them now. I spoke hastily awhile ago— we are all apt to do that you know, when we are a little out of humor —I ask your pardon?

Mack. I spoke rather hasty myself, Guy, so I guess we are about even on that score—but this business we had planned out for to-night, about Grey's dust, are we to drop that or not?

Guy. By no means, if everything is all in shape, why not carry out our plans?

Mack. That suits me, and as it is near eleven now, let's start at once—Toomstone seems unusually quiet to-night, I wonder what can be the cause? Here (*hands mask*) put that on, we may meet some one and we better keep on the safe side.

Guy. Ah! Mack, those masks are a good idea, they may save us a great deal of trouble.   (*put on masks*

   Mack. Now then, are you armed?

   Guy. Yes, I always am.

   Mack. Then come on.   (*exeunt, L.*

Enter, NELL., R., 1 E., *rifle in hand.*

Nell. Ah! you old stick in the mud. (*points L.*) I'm after you. don't think that Charley Grey's dust is lying around loose just because Charley isn't here to protect it. If I don't give you a surprise to-night, my name ain't Nell.   (*exit, L.*

Enter, EBONY, R., 1 E., *cautiously and badly scared; lights down gradually.*

   Ebony. Golly! I'd rather sleep to-night dan look fer thieves, but boss Charley's dust gotter be pertected and I'm de feller what can do it. (*looks L., trembling*) Golly! what am dat? I wish I hadn't come, I allers get sick when I'm by myself after night. (*slight noise R.*) Boss, am dat you? Golly! I wish I hadn't come. (*nervous— gun discharged off R.*) Fo' de good Lo'd sake; (*drops on knees*) now I lay me down ter—ter—ter—now I lay me down—down—I golly dis child is hoo-dood sho', now I lay me—(*looks R.*) lay me—lay me —(*looks over shoulder, etc.—business*) don't believe it was anything after all.   (*noise L., hands up—works mouth—says nothing*

   Nell. (*out L., calls softly*) Ebony!

   Ebony. (*raises quickly*) I golly, Miss Nell dat you? Dis child's glad to see you, I tells you. (*bravely*) Jerry Mack, de avenger am on yer track. (*flourishes white-wash brush*) Hi! dare Miss Nell, I golly, wait for dis chile.   (*runs out L., 1 E.*

Enter, JOE, R E.

   Joe. Well, of all the goin's on in Toomstone that I've seed fer some time dod burn my tarnal eye-sight; if this don't beat me. Here I find Nell out on the street with her rifle, likes if she was a lookin' fer some one, and that little speciman of Africa follerin' long after her, and here it's almost midnight. Wonder what they are after. I think I'll kinder hang around awhile and see, and ef there's a scrimmage comes up, why dod burned ef old Joe don't take a hand in it. Them's my sentiments persactly, and I don't give a cuss. I wish I had a chaw of dogleg tobacker ter keep me company, but dod burn the difference, here goes fer finden out what these "cur'os" proceedin's mean. Them's my sentiments jist ter a dod, and I don't give a cuss.   (*exit, L., 1 E.*

   SCENE III.—CHARLEY GREY'S *Cabin.*

Enter, MACK and GUY *cautiously with dark lantern—looks around, etc.*

   Mack. It's all right old man, no one there and no one has seen us, now let's hustle and get the dust and be off.

Guy. I'm your man for the dust. Where do you suppose he has it hid?

Mack. It's in one corner of his cabin, I don't know which one, you look in one and I'll look in the other.

Guy. All right, keep your eyes peeled now, we don't want anyone to slip up on us.

Mack. I'll keep a sharp look out and you do the same. (MACK L., *on knees,* GUY R., *on knees, they search. Business as long as the audience will stand it)* Thunder! there's nothing here. *(moves to* R.

Guy. There's nothing here either. *(moves to* L.*)* Ah!

Mack. What's the matter? Found anything?

Guy. You bet I have. Mack, look here.

Mack. *(goes* L. *quickly, kneels side of* GUY*)* Thunderation.

Enter, NELL, L., *covers* MACK *and* GUY *with rifle,* EBONY *sneaks in from* L., *trembling, kneels* L. C.

Guy. There's a deuced big bunch of it, Mack.

Mack. Let me lift it Guy. *(pause)* Thunder! there's three thousand if there' an ounce. We can't divide it here, come and let's get out of this—quick as possible.

Guy. That's my ticket, we can't move any too quick now.

(they rise, facing audience

Nell. Halt! (MACK *and* GUY *startled*) Drop that dust; Charley Grey is not here to protect his own, but his friends are. Throw up your hands! (GUY *and* MACK *make a blind rush out* R., NELL *shoots*

Ebony. Fo' de good Lo'd sake, dis chile is gone, I golly.

(exit, L., 1 E.

Enter, JOE, L., 2 E., *presents two revolvers.*

Joe. Hold on thare my beauty, drop that shootin' iron; (NELL *lowers rifle*) throw up two hands. (NELL *faces* JOE) What? dod burn my tarnal eyesight; Nell! you here in Charley Grey's cabin at midnight. Gal, what does this mean?

Nell. They were going to steal Charley's dust. *(points* R.*)* See! I was just in time to keep them from carrying it away.

Joe. Nell, you've got the grit, dod burned ef you ain't, put her thar' gal; *(hand out)* Joe's yer friend. You've got a heart bigger than a salt barrel. Them's my sentiments persactly, and I don't give a cuss.

QUICK CURTAIN.

END OF ACT II.

ACT III.

SCENE I.—BRANDON'S *rooms,* ARTHUR *seated* L., MRS. BRANDON *seated* L. C.

Mrs. Brandon. What is the matter with you this morning, Arthur, you seem more despondant than ever. I have noticed of late that you were worrying yourself over something; you must quit that, or you will certainly make yourself ill. Is it business trouble that is bothering you? Come confide in me, tell me what you are studying about.

Arthur. I was thinking about you, Julia.

Mrs. B. About me, and what about me?

Arthur. O! this country is so wild and rough, I have been thinking that it would be better for you—nor us both, if we were back at the old home. Just think, there is hardly a day passes here in Toomstone without a quarrel or a fight taking place, and often resulting fatally.

Mrs. B. But we have not done what we came here to do; you forget—

Arthur. Forget? No! Julia, I wish I could forget. I have worked hard with the one idea in view, and that to forget, but I have failed. I can never forget. It is true that we have established nothing, neither will we.

Mrs. B. But the anonymous letters we received, saying that we could learn something of the lost by coming here. Have you lost faith in them?

Arthur. Haven't we been here in Toomstone a year? And what have we learned? Nothing, absolutely nothing. The child is dead, long ere this. How many times have I lain awake the entire night, studying and brooding over the case. No! Julia, the child is dead.

Mrs. B. I have tried to bring myself to that belief, but I can not. I think that those anonymous letters did mean something. I feel that we shall yet see our child and be proud of her.

Arthur. Don't delude yourself with that idea, Julia; don't cherish that hope, for 'tis vain—useless.

Mrs. B. Arthur, do you know that this is her birthday, that seventeen years ago to-night she was stolen from us?

Arthur. Do I remember? Oh! only too well. Seventeen long miserable years, seventeen bleak, cheerless birthdays; if she was living to-day, she would be nineteen. What suspense for a father— (*looks at* JULIA) for a mother to be in. (*walks stage*) Yes, seventeen years ago to-night, our child—Gracie—was stolen from us, merely for revenge. What a fiend a man must be who will seek revenge by—

Mrs. B. No! do not think that Arthur, she was carried away by a roving band of Indians, which passed near us on that night. Everything went to prove that she was lost, seen wandering towards the camp of the Indians. I do not think that Fred Eldair—

Arthur. Fred Eldair was a man who would stop at nothing, Julia, when once his passion was aroused. When I detected him in stealing money from me, he swore to be revenged upon me. A great many men would have had him imprisoned, but he was young then and that was his first offense—he promised me to lead an upright and honest life, and on that promise I let him go. I can't help but think that he is the one who stole our child.

Mrs. B. 'Tis true that he disappeared at the same time Gracie did, but that proves nothing against him. I am sure it was the Indians who carried her off.

Arthur. Perhaps you are right, I hope you are. I don't like to wrong any man, but why has he kept himself hidden all these years?

Mrs. B. Why uncover the past? Let us strive to make it a blank, do not re-call those old memories, we have ourselves left, we will not grieve for our child, but think she is better off.

Arthur. O! Julia, what a comforter you are. If it had not been

for you, I believe I should have gone mad long ago. We have ourselves left, we will live for one another and think that all is for the
best. (*exit*, MRS. BRANDON

Enter, BESSIE GREY, R., 1 E.

Bessie. Mr. Arthur Brandon?

Arthur. That is my name—can I be of service to you?

Bessie. You are the banker of Toomstone?

Arthur. I can hardly be called a banker; however, I do some
banking business here merely to accommodate the miners.
(*both sit at table*

Bessie. We are alone, I presume?

Arthur. We are—please state your business.

Bessie. My name is Bessie Grey—I am Charley Grey's wife—I
arrived here in Toomstone last evening, and as Charley was over on
the "Divide," I stayed at the "Gold Dust Hotel." Every one in
Toomstone, was wild over the news that Charley had struck it rich,
that "Claim 96" was likely to prove the most valuable mine in this
camp. Exagerated stories were told of the amount of dust Charley
had secreted in his cabin.

Arthur. Ah! yes, I heard some of the absurd stories myself, to
the effect that Charley had gold dust pile l upon the floor of his cabin
a foot deep.

Bessie. Yes, that story and a great many others equally as ridic-
ulous, were circulated and were really believed by a number of
people of Toomstone, and last night, during Charley's absence, an
attempt was made to steal his dust, but the robbers were foiled by
the timely arrival of Nell. Charley had hid his dust in his cabin,
but he hadn't the amount that people thought he had, or anything
near it.

Arthur. Oh! certainly, the stories about Charley's good luck were
greatly exagerated, but the inhabitants of Toomstone are ready to
believe anything, if they hear the word "gold" mentioned in con-
nection with it.

Bessie. This morning Charley and I decided that it would not be
safe to keep the dust in his cabin any longer, and as we didn't want
anyone to know that we had move l it, and as I am a stranger here
in Toomstone, we decided that it would be best for me to bring it;
he said that you would put it in your safe and give me a certificate
of deposit. (*hands* ARTHUR *bag of gold*

Arthur. (*takes dust*) Oh! certainly, certainly, but as this is
merely an accommodation, I, of course, am not responsible—

Bessie. I understand Mr. Brandon, but Charley has all confidence
in your honesty.

Arthur. Ah! thank you—excuse me, I will lock the dust in the
safe. (*exit*, L., 2 E.

Bessie. There is one responsibility off of my mind, we will out-
wit the thieves of Toomstone yet.

Enter, GUY, R., 1 E., *looks around cautiously; sees* BESSIE *and slips
out* R., 1 E.

Re-enter, ARTHUR, L., 2 E.

Arthur. Under the circumstances, Mrs. Grey, I think that Charley has done the best thing he could do by placing the dust in my keeping, as his life would not be safe as long as he had the gold in his possession. (*writes*) Here is the certificate of deposit, (*hands paper*) and tell Charley that I hope his prosperity will not be short lived, but will hold up until he has massed a comfortable fortune.

Bessie. (*rises*) Thank you Mr. Brandon, and except our thanks for taking care of the dust for us, for we appreciate the favor—good morning.

Arthur. Ah! there's a business woman, and she has more refinement then I have seen since coming to Toomstone.

Enter, GUY, R., 1 E.

Guy. Ah! good morning Mr. Brandon; Lester is my name—Guy Lester. I suppose you know me by sight, if not personally. I called this morning to ask you a few questions; I believe that Charley Grey deposited some dust with you this morning?

Arthur. Then sir! your suppositions are wrong, I have had no dealings with Mr. Grey this morning, or at any previous time.

Guy. Then Grey's wife deposited the dust, did she?

Arthur. You are prying into business that does not concern you sir! and I decline to answer, go and ask that lady herself if you wish to know—I wish you good morning. (*turns to table*

Guy. (*clinches hands*) Arthur Brandon, you'll see the time when you will wish that you had told me what I wanted to know.

(*exit, R., 2 E.*

SCENE II.—Street.

Enter, PETERSON, L. E.

Peterson. I guess that would be a tetotal good speculation, if I could just find the right man, I'd trade him two barrels of apple sass for a square meal, and think I'd made a darned good bargain. I've got to have something to eat pretty soon, or I'll blow away, or wilt right down like a cabbage leaf in July. I'm just like the atmosphere —one big vacuum—if I was to stumble I'd break into corn stalks and bean poles; but I'd just like to see how much grub I could store away. I feel just perpendicularliy flabergasted, tetotally so. If things don't change for the better soon, I guess I will borrow six pence, buy a rope and hang myself. If I don't get something to eat before another week rolls around, there won't be enough of me left to make a grease spot. I'd like to put my feet under some man's table, if I wouldn't make a tetotal cleaning. I swear I'd split up the table legs for tooth picks.

Enter, EBONY, R. E.

Ebony. Black yere boots, shine 'em up. Hello! dar, you don't look like you'd seen pay dirt fer sometime.

Peterson. Say, boy, boy, go way, don't talk to me. I am offering more inducements now, for a square meal, than any other living man. I offer two barrels of apple sass for a good dinner.

Ebony. Are you hungry?

Peterson. Hungry? Boy, if I don't get something to eat soon, I'll be a tetotal wreck.

Ebony. You ort to been with me awhile ago, boss; I had de finest dinner—roast duck, roast turkey, roast goose, roast everything.

Peterson. Ah! boy, boy, boy. *(in agony*

Ebony. And all kinds of vegetables, roast vegetables.

Peterson. What a tetotal good dinner that was, wasn't it?

Ebony. You bet! and we had pie and cake.

Peterson. Say boy, where did you eat that dinner? Was there any scraps left?

Ebony. Yes, but dey done throwd 'em out to de chickens.

Peterson. Say, you take me down there and I'll pick around while anyway.

Ebony. What will you give me to told yer where you can get a good dinner?

Peterson. I've got four barrels of apple sass to home, the best apple sass that was ever make in Vermont, and I'll just be tetotally sizzled if I don't give you a whole barrel of that apple sass, if you will help me to get a square—rectangular—parolelogranical meal. There now, ain't that fair?

Ebony. Well now, here's de way fer you to get de dinner—you go down to de "Gold Dust Hotel" and tell old Mack, dat Charley Grey done give you a paper fer to carry to his wife, and if he will give you a square meal you'll done give him de paper, and I'll bet all de bri-tles out'en my shoe brush, you git's de grub. *(exit, L.*

Peterson. Now that's what I call a tetotally perpendicular good speculation; here goes for the grub. *(starts, R.*

Enter, BESSIE, R. E., *meets* PETERSON, R. C.

Say female, I am just about flabergasted, and I'd be tetotally oblig to you for a little information. Can you tell me—

Bessie. *(snapishly)* No! I can't—I'm no guide post. *(exit, ..*

Peterson. *(looks after her)* Squashed, tetotally; I guess I'll walk *(exit, R.*

SCENE III.—MACK's saloon.—MACK and GUY at bar.

Guy. I tell you Mack, that was a narrow escape for us both; I heard that bullet sing as it passed my ear, and when I seen Nell raise her rifle, I thought it would be "all day" with one of us any way, for you know she is a dead sure shot.

Mack. You bet I do, Guy, and when I looked around and seen her standing there with her rifle at her shoulder, I would have taken two cents for my chances of life and thought I was making big money I tell you old man, if she had pulled an inch lower, I'd passed in my checks. How do you suppose it happened that she was there anyway?

Guy. Well now you've got me Mack—I haven't the faintest suspicion, and what do you suppose ever caused her to miss that shot? For you know as well as I do, that she could have hit one of us if she had wanted to. Do you think she recognized us, or knew that we were going to Grey's cabin after his dust?

Mack. Thunder! no, she didn't know anything about it, and she never recognized us either—she couldn't—for you know we had our masks on. She just happened by Grey's cabin and heard us make a noise and came in to see what it was. But it is a little strange about her being there at midnight, isn't it? But then Nell is a strange girl, she is just as liable to be in one place as another.

Guy. Yes, and she happened to be just at the right place to spoil all of our plans everytime, Mack.

Mack. Yes, seems that way, but we could have got away with the dust that night, if you had not dropped it. Why didn't you hold on to it?

Guy. Hold on to nothing! I tell you, when I look around and see a rifle barrel pointed at me, with Nugget Nell behind it, and Nugget Nell's eye looking along the barrel like this, (*imitates*) I'll drop anything; I am not courting death yet awhile.

Mack. Thunder! but Nell did give me a shock last night. Honestly, I wouldn't have been any more surprised if I had seen Charley Grey standing there.

Guy. Or Charley's wife.

Mack. Ah! Guy, there's a woman we've got to watch.

Guy. You are just right we have Mack, and we can't watch her any too close either; she is a cute one I tell you.

Mack. Yes, she can take care of herself and her husband, and three or four other fellows like Grey.

Guy. My opinion is, that if she stays here in this camp for six months, the counterfeiters of Toomstone, will have to "fold their tents and gently steal away."

Mack. (*goes behind bar*) Here, (*sets bottle on bar*) take something, we must brace up some way—there is other work before us yet—come on and drink with me; this isn't the best, but then—

Enter, PETERSON, R., 1 E.

Peterson. I guess I can worry some of it down and be tetotally obliged to you in the bargain.　　　　(*reaches for bottle*

Mack. (*jerks bottle back*) Don't get too fast!

Peterson. Why! ain't you going to give me a drink?

Mack. I don't see that I am under any obligation to, sir!

Peterson. Now, that's what I call down right, tetotal selfishness in you. Say, I'll trade you a half barrel of apple sass for a drink—

Mack. No sir! I sell this whiskey for money.

Peterson. Well, that's the same way I sell my apple sass. Say, maybe you could loan me ten dollars and take your pay out in apple sass. I've got four barrel of the best apple sass—

Mack. No sir! I don't want to invest in any apple sass. Say, do you see that sign? (*points to sign over bar*—"*Treat—Trade or Travel*"

Peterson. (*reads*) "Treat—Trade or Travel"—well, you won't treat and I've offered you a perpendicular good trade—now that apple sass of mine (MACK *and* GUY *talk, pay no attention to* PETERSON) can't be beat, I tell you, it was made by one of the best cooks in Hillsborough county, Vermont—I mean Polly Ann Spriggins—she that used to be Polly Ann Flint before she was married—her and I are kinder related like—now her father, old Jebedil Flint, and my mother's great uncle were cousins—so you see we are bound together by the tie of consinganity. Now when Polly Ann married Jeddediah Spriggins—you see he had been married before, and she was his second wife. His first wife was taken with the cramps and went off kinder sudden like—she ate thirty-eight raw turnips one day and they didn't agree with her. Everybody said that Jeddediah made a tetotal good speculation when he married Polly Ann, 'cause Jeddediah wasn't worth nothing. He had forty acres of the worst land in Vermont. That land was so tetotal poor that you couldn't raise a disturbance on it. That farm was nothing but a big bunch of sand—it was a perpendicular fine place to scour knives, though—but as I was saying about Polly Ann—(*looks around an l sees* MACK *and* GUY *are paying no attention to him*) squashed tetotally. (*goes to table, sits down and sets grip on top of table*) Well, I'm just flabergasted, tetotally so. A fellow that's as backward and bashful as I am, oughtn't to be this far away from home.

Guy. (*points to* PETERSON) What do you call it, Mack?

Mack. I don't know. I'll investigate. (*goes* R. C.) Say, who are you anyway?

Peterson. I'm little Peter Peterson, from Peterville, Vermont I've got four barrels of the best apple sass—

Mack. Hold on! never mind that! What are you doing out here?

Peterson. Come out for my health, and it I could sell that apple sass—

Guy. Oh! let loose of the "apple sass," you don't look as if you found very much health.

Peterson. No! the air don't agree with me—but that apple sass—

Mack. Hold on! Say, did you expect to live on air?

Peterson. From what I heard about this country, I 'sposed I could and keep teto ally fat too. If the air had agreed with me, I figger t at I would weigh a little over seven hundred pounds now, but as it didn't agree with me, I only weigh about forty-two pounds. I am offering two whole barrels of apple sass—

Guy. How much longer are you going to talk about that "apple sass?"—

Peterson. It's a tetotal No. 1 good apple sass, and I can afford to talk about it—now this apple sass that—

Mack. Oh! hold on. Say, what did you come down here for?

Peterson. Why, Charley Grey gave me a paper to take to his wife, and I thought, maybe you'd give me a tetotal good dinner, if I'd give you the paper and throw in some apple sass—

Guy. Break off the "apple sass"—we don't want the paper.

Peterson. Wouldn't give me the dinner if I was to throw in one-half barrel of apple—

Mack. No! not if you was to throw in a barrel and a half.

Peterson. Well, am I to be tetotally swindled out of my dinner, with all my apple sass on hand? (MACK *and* GUY *both laugh*) This ain't no laughing matter, if I don't eat something pretty soon, I'll be a tetotal wreck.

Guy. (*gets sack of crackers behind bar*) Here, try these.

Peterson. (*takes sack*) Say, that will make a tetotal rectagular kind of a meal, won't it? Now, if I had some of that apple sass. Say, is there any water to go with these?

Guy. No sir! not a drop, you must eat them dry.

Peterson. Well, I can just do it. I'll eat the sack if you say so.

(*seated*

Enter, NELL, R., 3 E.

Nell. Hello! Guy. (*sees* PETERSON) What have you got there?

Mack. 'Tend bar awhile, Nell; come on Guy, let's walk dowr street and see if we can't find Grey.   (*exit, L., 1 E.*

Guy. Don't let that fellow have a drop of water, Nell.
                                                (*exit, L.,] E.*

Nell. All right!   (*behind bar. idly throwing dice*

Peterson. That's a perpendicular fine girl. I wonder if she has any objection- to matrimony. (*rises and leans against bar, facing the audience—business*) Miss. there's something laboring on the upperpart of my disposition, which I'd like tetotally well to promulgate.

Nell. (*throwing dice*) Two aces and a pair of sixes. Good throw.

Peterson. (*aside*) I don't seem to interest her. (*aloud*) Miss—ahem—Miss.

Nell. Well, what do you want? You can't work this bar for free drinks, understand that?

Peterson. Say, don't you want to buy four barrels of nice apple sass? I'll sell 'em dirt cheap.

Nell. No! I don't. Say, why don't you introduce yourself?

Peterson. I will, and when you get acquainted with me, you'll think I'm a tetotal perpendicular kind of a fellow too. My name is Peterson—Peter Ulyses Peterson.

Nell. Well Peterson, I'll shake you the box for the drinks.

Peterson. I never gambled with a girl before, but let 'er sliver.

Nell. (*throws dice*) There, beat four sixes.

Peterson. (*throws*) Three fives—say, that's the first equine on me. ain't it?

Nell. You owe me ten cents. (PETERSON *goes through pocket*) Well, hurry up, give me ten cents, or Mack will come in and think I am doing business on credit.

Peterson. (*searches clothes*) Say, I ain't got ten cents, take it out in apple sass, won't you? (NELL *turns away disgusted*) Say, be you engaged?

Nell. What?

Peterson. Did you ever experience the tender passion of love, that great pent up fire that will glow and smoulder in spite of you, until you think that you'll just tetotally sizzle?

Nell. No!

Peterson. Well, I have, I'm just tetotally scorched into a cinder now, and love is the cause of it—say, you'll be pretty well off one of these days, won't you?

Nell. I am pretty well off now.

Peterson. Well, so am I—that is to say, I will be when my aunt Huldi dies. I took an inventory of her effects last spring, and I find that she has two acres of land under water in South Carolina, besides eighteen dollars and five cents in cash on hand, and enough clothes to last her, her natural life time; that is, if it ain't spun out too tetotal long. Now, I think that it would be a perpendicular good speculation for us—you and I—to hitch up and wade down the stream of life together, don't you?

Nell. No! I don't.

Peterson. That is to say, you reject my suit?

Nell. You don't call that a suit, do you?

Peterson. I mean, that you don't feel matrimonially inclined toward the afore said Peterson—meaning me.

Nell. No! I don't, when I marry I want a *man*, not a shadow—understand?

Peterson. (*turns and sits at table—aside*) Another speculation tetotally busted (*aloud*) Wouldn't change your mind, I reckon, if I would throw in two barrels of apple sass?

Enter, MACK, GUY *and* CHARLEY, L., 1 *and* 2 E.

Mack. Now boys, let's hustle and get up a nice, quiet little game. (*sees* PETERSON) Hello! you here yet? Didn't I show you that sign awhile ago? (*exit,* NELL

Peterson. Well, I can't get a trade out of anybody around here. (*to* CHARLEY) Could you make me a small loan on four barrels of apple sass?

Chas. No! I'm not dealing in "apple sass" now.

Guy. Hurry up Mack, and get those chairs around that table and let's get to work. (MACK *gets chair, etc.,* GUY *goes behind bar*) Here take something, Charley.

Chas. No! I never drink before going into a game.

Peterson. You seem to be a tetotal perpendicular kind of a fellow, I'll drink with you. (*steps up to bar,* GUY *puts bottle behind bar and walks to table*) Another speculation busted.

Mack. All right, come on boys, sit down. (*they sit down—business*

Chas. Go on and deal, Mack. (MACK *deals*

Peterson. Wait! wait! where's my chair? I'm in that game.

Guy. You are not going to play in this game.

Peterson. Yes, I am too. (*kneels side of table*

Mack. All right boys, there's your cards.

Peterson. Wait! wait! where's my crackers? (*goes and gets them off bar and gets chair*) Here goes for a tetotal speculation.

Mack. Well, what are you doing?

Guy. I stay.

Chas. I see you myself.

Mack. Well, I am along with you boys.

Peterson. You seem to be a perpendicular kind of a crowd, I guess I'll stay too.

Mack. Cards?

Guy. Give me the three cards on top.

Chas. Bury that top one, Mack, and give me two.

Peterson. Give me three more kings, I've got one.

Guy. Hold on there! you haven't discarded yet; wait Mack, how many are you going to throw away?

Peterson. Four, the others are all three spots, I don't want them.

Chas. Give him four cards, Mack—now then.

Guy. Well, I'll chance five dollars any way.

Chas. I have a pretty good hand, I raise you five.

Mack. I pass out.

Peterson. I bet a barrel of apple sass—

Guy. Hold on! this game is for money, only.

Peterson. So is my apple sass.

Mack. You've got to bet money if you play in this game.

Peterson. Well, then I bet five.

Guy. All right, I call you.

Chas. I've got three queens.

Mack. Thunderation!

Guy. They are not large enough, I have four aces.

Peterson. I've won the money! I've won the money! (*jumps up*

Guy. What have you got?

Peterson. I've got three pairs—two duces, two fives and two jacks.

Guy. That hand's no good, you've got too many cards, you did not discard enough. You owe me ten dollars.

Peterson. How much?

Guy. Ten dollars.

Peterson. What for?

Guy. Why! for this hand that we just played. Come, hand it over.

Peterson. Say, I'm tetotally broke; take it out in apple sass, won't you? How much did he loose. (*points to* CHARLEY

Mack. Why, he lost ten dollars.

Peterson. How much did he loose? (*points to* MACK

Guy. Why, he passed out.

Peterson. Well, why the tetotal thunder, didn't I pass out?

Mack. (*presents revolver*) That's what you are going to do right now.

Peterson. (*steps back*) Hold on! hold on! I'll leave. I'll pass out. (*points East*) Is that the way to Vermont?

Mack. Yes sir! that's the way to Vermont.

Peterson. Hillsborough county?

Mack. Yes!

Peterson. Petersburgh?

Mack. Yes sir! now you get!

Peterson. That's where I am going—Petersburgh, Hillsborough county, Vermont. If you ever need any of my apple sass—

Guy. O! kill him Mack, why don't you shoot him?

Peterson. There's another speculation busted—say, that will be a tetotal nice little walk over to Vermont, won't it?

Mack. (*starts for him*) Say, are you going, or—

Peterson. I'm going. Good-by boys, good-by. (*exit*, L., *slowly*

Mack. That fellow is the hardest one to get rid of, I've seen for some time.

Chas. Why didn't you kick him out a long time ago, Mack?

Guy. That's a game that two can play at, and he is about as big as Mack is—Mack don't take no risks, do you Mack?

Mack. Let's get to work boys and finish this game.

(*chairs to table, all seated*

Enter, PETERSON, L. E.

Peterson. Say, do you know of any one else that wants to walk over to Vermont? I'd like company.

Mack. No sir! I don't. Now you get out of here.

Peterson. I am going—Petersburgh, Hillsborough county, Vermont. Good-by boys. (*exit*, L.

Mack. If you ever show your face in here again—

Guy. Mack, you've got an elephant on your hands, that fellow intends to stay with you.

Chas. He won't come back again—here let's get to playing, I want to win back that ten if I can—whose deal is it?

Enter, PETERSON, L. E., MACK *grabs him by throat.*

Peterson. Look out! be tetotally careful, that's my "jugler."

Mack. Hang your jugler! Didn't I tell you awhile ago, what I would do if you came in here again?

Guy. Now then, what the deuce do you want?

Peterson. (*points to grip on bar*) I want my trunk.

Mack. Well, you get it and get out of here.

Chas. And if you come back here again, I shall take it upon myself to kick you out in the street.

Peterson. All right—I'm going now—if you see anybody that wants to buy some tetotal fine apple sass—(Guy *rises*) Good-by boys, good-by.   (*exit,* L., *hurriedly*

Guy. Now then, let's have the game out—deal Charley.

Charley *deals, they play the hand, talk ad lib.; work it as long as audience will stand it.*

Enter, Bessie, L. E.

Bessie. Charley Grey, what are you doing here? Trying to loose what dust you have? Come and let's go home. Come on now!

Chas. All right! just as quick as I play this hand out; go on, I'll be there—give me three cards, Mack.

Bessie. No! you come with me, I won't move a step unless you go too; these fellows will cheat you out of all the dust you have. Come on!

Mack. Why, Mrs. Grey, this little game is just for pastime; of course there is some money up, but not enough—

Bessie. You shut up! I wasn't talking to you, you can't soft-soap me.

Enter, Ebony, R., 1 E.

Ebony. 'Caus, I golly, she don't use soap, do you?

Bessie. You little black imp.   (*makes a dive for him*

Ebony. (*dodges her*) I golly, boys, look out for storm · weather, fer she's got her skates on. It would take five aces and a "raizor" to beat dat hand, so it would, I golly.   (*exit,* L., 1 E.

Bessie. (*takes hold of chair,* Carley *rises*) Now, come on and let's go; don't stay here and associate with that old thief, (*points to* Mack) he would steal anything he could get his hands on, (Guy *laughs*) and you too, I mean both of you.   (*starts,* L., 2 E.

Guy. Come back sometimes and we will finish that game, Charley.

Bessie. No! he won't either; if he does, I'll follow him with a broom. Charley Grey has a wife that will take care of him, he'll do as I say.   (*exit, both,* L., 2 E., Mack *and* Guy *laugh*

Enter, Peterson, L., 1 E.

Peterson. Now, there's another perpendicular good speculation tetotally busted, I might say.

Mack. (*sees* Peterson) Well, I'll swear, if that ain't cheek personified.

Guy. Didn't we tell you awhile ago, to never come in here again.

Peterson Yes but say, is that the way to Vermont?   (*points East*

Mack. Yes, that's the way to Vermont.

Peterson. Well, I walked up that way about a mile and a half, but I never saw anything of it.

Guy. See here, I am going to count five, and if you are not out of here when I get through, you will cease to exist; now then, one—two—three—four—fi—

Peterson. Four and one-half time. Say, don't rush me out so fast, I think I see a tetotal good speculation down here. I've got a trade up. I can get a sway backed mule for three barrels of apple sass. (MACK *and* GUY *push him out* L.

Guy. (*seated*) Well Mack, what do you think of Charley Grey's wife now?

Mack. (*seated*) I think she will run Toomstone to suit herself.

Guy. So do I, and if we do anything about Grey's dust, we will have to work lively, I tell you. She deposited the dust with old Brandon this morning.

Enter, BELL, L., 3 E., *stops and listens.*

Mack. Thunder! is that so? Well, that's better for us, old Brandon is keeping dust for several of the miners, and we can go up there to-night and blow that safe open easy enough and get well payed for the work too. (*sees* BELL) Ah! eavesdropping again are you, curse you. (*jerks her to* C., *exit,* GUY, R., 1 E.

Bell. I didn't intend to overhear, but I couldn't help it, and the words I overherd are terrible. Jerry, don't do that, give it up for my sake if not your own.

Mack. Shut up! didn't I tell you once, that if I caught you at this sneaking game again, I'd cure you of it; now then, I am going to keep my word. (*gets whip behind bar*

Bell. You can whip me Jerry, if you want to, but don't be a thief, a "safe breaker." (*kneels*) See, on my knees I ask you to give up this wild scheme.

Mack. Get up! (BELL *rises*) I used to whip niggers, and I'll show you that I haven't forgot how to use the lash yet. I'll learn you to mind your own affairs. (*strikes*) You dare to scream and I'll put a bullet through your treacherous heart. (*strikes*

Bell. (*kneels*) O! Jerry! Jerry! have some mercy.

Enter, PETERSON, L. E.

Peterson. I say, that's a tetotal darnation shame. I'll give you a barrel of apple sas, if you'll quit.

Mack. Get out of here, curse you.

MACK *strikes* PETERSON, *who runs out* L., *yelling, then strikes* BELL, *she screams.*

Bell. O! Jerry! Jerry! quit, for heaven's sake, stop!

Enter, NELL, R. E., *raises rifle.*

Nell. Jerry Mack stop that!

(MACK *stops and looks at* NELL, BELL *on knees* R. C.

SCENE IV.—Street.

Enter, PETERSON, L. E.

Peterson. Gosh all hemlock, bald hornets and yaller jackets, but that fellow can use a whip. If he was back in Vermont, he would make a tetotal fortune in less than a month, driving an ox team. This is a perpendicular fine kind of a place, but I don't see any opening for me. It's going to be a tetotal long walk over to Vermont, but as the old saying is—"a light heart and a thin pair of pants get merrily through the world." If times don't improve, or I don't get something to eat before another week rolls around, I'll put a postage stamp on my ear and send myself through by mail; that would be a tetotal good speculation, if I could find some man that I could trade two barrels of my apple sass too for a stamp.

Enter, MACK, L. E., *gesticulating wildly.*

Good-by, good-by. (*exit,* R., *quickly*
Mack. Thunderation! if I have to face Nell's rifle once more, my nerves will be shattered. I don't see why she can't mind her own affairs and let me alone. That's twice she has come in on me. I am almost ready to believe that she is watching me. If she is, I will have my hands full to keep clear of her, and there's Grey's wife—curse her, I wish she was away from here, she beats anything I ever saw—

Enter, EBONY, L. E.

Ebony. I golly, she does, don't she? Say, let me shine yer shoes boss, ain't made a nickel to-day.
Mack. Say, you little black cuss, what made you pilot Grey's wife down to the "Gold Dust" and brake up that game for? She is worse than a powder magazine.
Ebony. I didn't send her down dar.
Mack. Yes, you did too!
Ebony. No! I didn't neither. Let me told yer 'bout dat—you see she was a walkin' down de street and she done see me and she says, "here, can you done told me where boss Charley am," and I say "no" and she say—"nigger, do you done 'spose he's down to de 'Gold Dust'," and I done told her dat I 'spect not, and she say, don't you go fer to lie to me you little brack cuss, and with dat she made one grab for dis child's wool, but I wasn't dar boss. I tell you, I was clean gone outen sight. I golly boss, when she came fer me I was scared, I thought dis child done hoo dooed, sho'.
Mack. That woman beats the devil.
Ebony. Dat's just right boss, sho'. I done told yer she's way outen sight. De debil needn't watch Toomstone any longer, not while she's here. (*look* R.) Hi dar boss Charley, lemme done shine yer shoes, ain't made a nickel to-day. (*exit,* R.
Mack. I'll swear, I don't know whether to think that little black imp is lying to me or not. I suppose I'll have to take it for granted, that he told me the truth. I'll hunt up Guy and speak to him about it.

MACK *starts* R., JOE *enters* R. E.

Why, hollo! Joe, shake hands old man—
Joe. No sir! dod burn you Jerry Mack, your too ornery to shake
hands with old Joe. Them's my sentiments, persactly.
Mack. Why! what in thunder's the matter now?
Joe. The matter is just this, dod burn you, I know you, Fred
Eldair.
Mack. (*startled*) What?   (*recoils* L. C
Joe. I've read the little book that you kept locked up in your desk,
I know all about Nell, dod burn you, and I'll tell old—
Mack. Curse you, don't you mention that name.
Joe. I will too. Them's my sentiments and I don't give a cuss.
Mack. Curse you, you will never tell that story to any one else.
                                                    (*draws knife*
Joe. I will! I'll tell Nell and I'll tell Arthur Brandon.
Mack. You cursed traitor!

Rushes on him, stabs him; he falls back as NELL *enters; she catches
him as he sinks to the floor.*

Nell. O! Joe! Joe! he has killed you.
Joe. (*raises on elbow*) You'll regret this to your dying day, Fred,
for I am your brother.
Nell. (*helps* JOE *to rise*) Blast your eyes, Jerry Mack, you've
killed the best friend I had. I'll get even with you for this.
                                                    (*helps* JOE *out* R.
Mack. (C., *speaks slow*) My-brother, I-have-killed-my-brother
and we were playmates together. My brother, who—

Enter, GUY, L. E.

Guy. Hello! Mack. what's the matter with you—you look all
shaken up—have you seen a ghost?
Mack. I—I—I don't know Guy, I hope so—I—I—
Guy. You've been patronizing your own bar, Mack.
Mack. No! Guy, I—I don't feel "like myself."
Guy. Well, if you will walk around a while, you'll soon be "yourself" again. Let's move lively now an I pay a visit to old Brandon
and go through that iron box of his. I am anxious to see the inside
of it. Remember Mack, "Claim 96" may be the reward to-night,
and I have everything all ready.   (*exit,* L.
Mack. (*starts* L.) All right Guy, I'm—I'm a little nervous now,
but I'll be all right directly.   (*exit,* L., *slowly*

Enter, EBONY, R. E.

Ebony. Hello! old stick in the mud is gone. I golly, didn't I
done hoo-doo him with dat big lie 'bout Mrs. Grey? Dis chile is way
outen sight, I tole yer.

Enter, NELL, R. E., *rifle in hand.*

Hello! dar Miss Nell; golly, what you goin' to you?
Nell. I am going to put a hole through Jerry Mack's heart. He
stuck a knife in old Joe a while ago.   (*exit,* L.
Ebony. For the good Lo'd sake, you don't told me so? Well. I

always like to be in at the death. Hi! dar, Miss Nell, wait for dis
chile. (*exit*, L.

SCENE V.—Room in MR. BRANDON'S *house; stage dark, safe* L.
upper corner. Enter, GUY *and* MACK *masked, with burglar tools—
look around cautiously.*

Guy. Let's get to work old man, the coast is clear and we can't
afford to fool away any time here.
Mack. Have you got everything—the powder?
Guy. Yes, everything, let's hurry. (*they go to work on safe*

Enter, MRS. BRANDON, R., 1 E.

Mrs. B. I cannot sleep, I have tried, but in vain; sleep will not
visit my eyes to-night. I am filled with a foreboding of evil to us or
to someone through us. I have tried to banish the thought, but I
can not.

Heavy explosion to R. E., *as* GUY *and* MACK *blow open safe;* MRS.
BRANDON *screams,* GUY *rises.*

Guy. You got the dust Mack, I'll take care of her. (*catches* MRS.
BRANDON *by throat, she falls,* GUY *stabs her—rises*) Are you ready,
Mack?
Mack. Yes, yes, I've got it; quick, let's go.
(*both exit,* R., 1 E., *hurriedly*

Enter, ARTHUR, L., 3 E.

Arthur. What can be the meaning of the noise I heard.

Enter, NELL, R., 3 E., *rifle in hand, stands till curtain drops.*

I could have sworn that I heard a woman scream. (*sees* MRS. BRAN-
DON) What's this? (*kneels*) My God! it's Julia, what villain can
have done this? Julia! Julia! look up, speak just one word, whose
work is this? Julia! Julia! O! God, she's dead and I am left alone.
(*head bowed*

CURTAIN.

END OF ACT III.

ACT IV.

*SCENE I.—*MACK'S *saloon—*NELL *leaning against bar,* L., *playing
with her revolver, rifle lying across bar.*

Enter, EBONY, L., 1 E.

Ebony. I golly, Miss Nell, I just believe you naturally love dem
ar' gun's, you'se always foo in' with 'em.
Nell. They are the best friends I've got, Ebony.
Ebony. Golly, ain't you 'fraid of 'em?
Nell. Afraid? Ha! ha! (*laughs*) not much I ain't. Most girls
have dolls to play with when they are small, but I never had, I never

had anything to amuse myself with but guns, and revolvers, and knives. I've grown to love them—but how's Toomstone this morning—quiet?

Ebony. No sir! dey are badly flustercated now, I tole yer.

Nell. Well, two murders in one night is enough to excite even Toomstone and all it's natives.

Enter, BELL, R., 2 E.

Bell. Toomstone seems unusually excited this morning. Nell, what is the matter?

Nell. O! nothing, I guess.

Bell. Have you seen anything of Jerry, this morning?

Nell. No! (*picks up rifle*) but I'd like to.

Bell. He never came in at all last night. There must be something wrong. I can't help thinking there is some terrible calamity about to befall us, everything seems wrong this morning.

Enter, OFFICER, L., 1 E.

Officer. Nell, you are my prisoner.

Bell. What?   (*recoil* R. C.

Officer. Let me see your hands. (NELL *holds out hand, he handcuffs her*) I arrest you for the murder of Julia Brandon.

Bell. O! Nell! Nell! has it really come to this. Did you do that?

Nell. No! but I know who did, and I'll make it warm for them when I get out.

Bell. O! don't take Nell away, don't, she never committed a crime in her life; let her go, take me.

Officer. Madam, I am simply doing my duty. The charge of murder is against her, if she is innocent and can prove it, all well and good, but I must take her to the station house.

Ebony. I say, it's er shame, I golly, and I can lick yer too.

Officer. Come, let us be moving.   (*start* L.

Bell. Good-by Bell, I'll be back soon.

Bell. O! Nell, I can't let you go (*throws her arm around* NELL) alone, I shall go with you.

OFFICER *pushes* BELL *aside and exit,* L. *with* NELL. BELL *seated crying.*

Ebony. (*following* OFFICER) Coward! coward! 'fraid to take any body of your size—why don't you take a man. Just tackle me, I golly. I'll stay with you, Nell.   (*exit,* L.

SCENE II.—Street.

Enter, MAJOR, L. E.

Maj. Be gad, sah. I can't say that I like this diabolical country, they are too free with their "sticker;" dang a man that fights with a knife anyhow. Why don't they choose something more modern like this, (*shows revolver*) Be gad, there's "old never fail," just give me a little gin and peppermint, and "old never fail" and I can lick all the western desperates that get their washing done in this camp. Be gad, I'm Major Dolittle, from Kentucky, sah; used to own one

hundred niggers. I sign my name with an X, and be gad, I'll go
and get some gin and peppermint.   (*start*, R.

Enter, EBONY, R. E.

Ebony. O-o-o-o, etc.   (*crying very loud*
Maj. Hello! there, gad boy, what's the matter? Say, I wouldn't
cry about it. (EBONY *cries louder*) Say, pickaninny, don't take it
so to heart. Brace up—come and go with me and get some gin and
peppermint. (*pause*) What's the matter, anyway?
Ebony. (*crying*) Dey've done been gone and tooken my girl off to
de jug-up, I golly.
Maj. What's that; took her where?
Ebony. (*crying*) Down to de—de—de jug-up.
Maj. I guess, be gad, that you mean the lock-up, don't you?
Ebony. Well, dey's all de same, jug-up and lock-up, ain't dey?
They've got her in jail anyhow.
Maj. Well, who is the girl that's in jail?
Ebony. Why, our Nell, I golly, and I'm goin' to get her out too.
Maj. Gad boy, she's the same girl that used to sell such diabolical
good gin and peppermint down to the "Gold Dust," ain't she?
Ebony. Dat's de girl and now dey's got her in de jug-up.
Maj. I'm Major Dolittle, from Kentucky, sah—I'll go and get
some gin and peppermint, and help you get the girl out.
Ebony. I golly, boss, if you'll done do dat dis chile will be way
outen sight, now I done tole yer.
Maj. Well, be gad boy, I'll do it. You run down the street and
wait un il I come. (EBONY *exit*, L.) Gad, I'll annihilate 'em; (*searches!
pockets* where's my annihilator? Come out here "old never fail."
(*draws revolver*) Be gad, sah, you've got to wade through blood—
becau e I'm Major Dolittle, from Kentucky, sah, and I'll go and get
some gin and peppermint. (*start* R.) Gad, Major, you are gifted
with an immen e amount of courage.

Enter, JENNIE, R. E., *sees* MAJOR *and tries to pass him hurriedly.*

Hold on there! be gad, I believe I know you.
Jen. I don't allow strangers to accost me in the street.
Maj. Well, be gad, I don't think we a e strangers. Let me see
your hand, don't hold back, let's see your hand.
Jen. I don't know what you mean, but there's my hand.
Maj. Oh! I thought that we were acquainted. My old slave
brand, I recognize that "S", that stands for Slaves. Be gad, I've
found you at last, haven't I?
Jen. You are an entire stranger to me. Let loose ot my hand, or
I shall call for assistance.
Maj. Be gad, I'm from Kentucky; you don't work that dodge on
me. Don't you suppose I know my old slaves? Especially, when
they have the brand on their hands. O! I know you. Gad, I hate
niggers, 'specially runaway niggers; I've a great notion to take you
back to the plantation and set you to work. What made you run
away.
Jen. O! that life was too terrible, we couldn't stay; but don't take
us back, we will do anything—anything but that, we have money
we will buy our freedom—
Maj. Gad, don't you know that the niggers are free?

Jen. But we will pay you anything you ask, if you will let us alone—to do as we please.

Maj. Where's that nigger brother of yours. I'd like to see the rascal. Be gad, I'd put a hole through that black heart of his, that you could throw a chinese bible throu' . Come out here "old never fail." (*draws revolver*) I'll tell everyone here in Toomstone, that you and your brother used to be slaves—runaway niggers, and you used to belong to Major Dolittle, of Kentucky. Be gad, sah, I hate niggers, 'specially runaway niggers. I've a notion to shoot a hole through both of your ears, so I will know you atter this.

Jen. O! don't, please don't, you couldn't be that cruel. Let us go and we will leave here and never cross your path again. We have been slaves, and branded with the mark, which we shall carry to the grave, but do not tell the miners that we were once slaves, don't be so inhuman—I beg you—more—I implore you—   (*about to kneel*)

Maj. Get up girl, I ain't no little tin God on wheels, you needn't kneel to me—you can go, for I'm dry, I'm going to get some gin and peppermint, be gad. I'll pay you and your brother a visit one of these days, and then I will settle accounts with you.   (*exit, R.*

Jen. (*draws dirk and slips after him*) Ah! I could kill you—yes, kill you. (*pause*) But no, there's been enough murder done in Toomstone for one night—(*looking R.*) but to be called "slave—runaway nigger," to have that thrown in my face—I shall go and tell Guy and put him on his guard.   (*exit, L.*

SCENE III.—MACK's *saloon,* BELL *seated* R. C., EBONY *standing* L. C., BELL *crying.*

Ebony. Now looky here, Mrs. Bell, don't you go fer to take on so bout dis hear. I tell yer things will come out all right yet. Nell never done gone kill no 'oman, now I done tole yer dat ar' gal did never do dat, don't I know her? I'm de feller what kin git her outen dat ar' old jug-up, and I golly, I'se goin' to do it too. I'll just git 'er big long pole and put dat pole under dat jug-up and den pull down and dat will just turn dat jug-up right up side down, den Mr. Jug-up fall all to pieces and Miss Nell come out, and den we will tell dem to go to de debil, and we will go to de "Gold Dust."

Bell. Why Ebony! that wouldn't do; you couldn't do that.

Ebony. Yes, I could too! Now I done tole yer dat a nigger can do a good deal, and den dat feller from Kaintuck' done told me he'd help. Goin' to git dat gal onten dat jug-up sho'.

Bell. But Ebony, if Nell escapes, that will go to prove that she did kill Mrs. Brandon, and then the Regulators would soon be atter her—we must do all we can to turn suspicion away from her. Ebony, we must work to get proof of her innocence, we must find out who made the charge against her. Who do you suppose did, Ebony?

Ebony. I golly, you'se got me clean outen sight, but maybe I can done find out.

Bell. If we could find out that—then we would have something to work on, a clue to go by, but it certainly was made for revenge by some enemy of her's.

Ebony. Dat's so, I golly, I wish I had hold of dat feller, I'd jerk forty-eleven different kinds of stuffing outen him.

Bell. I didn't know that she had an enemy; she **was a favorite** with every one in Toomstone.

Ebony. 'Specially me, I golly.

Bell. She has said something or done something that has made someone mad at her, and that person has brought this charge against her through malice.

Ebony. I golly, if I had him, I'd "mallet" him, I'd make him think he was hoo-dood, sho'.

Bell. All this trouble and excitement is causing my head to ache and whirl so that I do not know what to do, or which way to turn. O! Nell! Nell! why did this trouble have to come up?

(*breaking down*

Ebony. I golly, I knows what I'm goin' to do. I'm goin' to have a geolery all by myself, and d it's woat you'd better do too, and den you will feel better. (*turning*) I goily, dis nigger's eyes are leakin' now. (*exit*, R.

Bell. I don't know but Ebony is giving me good advice, and I will not give way as long as I can keep from it. I must keep my courage up now, if I possibly can. Jerry is in some trouble I know, or he would have been here long before this. If he has done what I overheard him and Guy Lester planning to do yesterday, and he is found out, and Nell in jail for a crime she never committed—O! what shall I do—no one to advise me—no one to help me. O! Nell! Nell! (*crying*

CURTAIN.

END OF ACT IV.

ACT V.

SCENE I—Street. Enter, MACK and GUY *from* L. E., *with* NELL, *whose hands are tied behind her, handkerchief tied over her mouth, she pulls back, etc—business.*

Mack. Come on! come on! There's no use to pull back, for you've got to go with us; hold on to her, Guy.

Guy. It won't do you any good to struggle, for you've got to go, you know too much about us.

Mack. We will take good care of you, Nell.

Guy. Yes, and take good care that you don't tell any one what you know, too. Hurry up Mack, we haven't any time to fool away here, some one may see us; if she won't walk, carry her.

(*they exit*, R., *draging* NELL *with them*

Enter, MAJOR, L. E.

Maj. Well, be gad, I'm stumped, the "Gold Dust" is shut up and I ain't got any gin and peppermint; wonder what's got the matter with Toomstone anyway. Be gad, I'm Major Dolittle, from Kentucky, and I'll have gin and peppermint or blood. Come out here "old never fail." (*draws revolver*

Enter, EBONY, L. E., *excited.*

Ebony. O! boss! boss! what you'se think? Dey've done gone and broken into de jug-up and carried Miss Nell off up the mountain along with Charley Grey's dust. For de good Lo'd sakes I—I—I—I golly!

Maj. Well, be gad, sah, I'll go and get some gin an l peppermint, and we will go and get her. I want to go up on the mountain anyway, got a runaway nigger up there that I want to see. We will take "old never fail," and be gad, sah, we will shoot out a path through them and get the girl. We wi l have her if we have to wade through blood, "old never fail" is always in the ring. I'll go and get some gin and peppermint, and then we'll go.

Ebony. Say, boss, can't you get her by yourself? I don't believe I want to go up dar'—I golly, I don't.

Maj. What's the matter nigger, 'fraid?

Ebony. N—n—no—ain't 'fraid, but I golly, I'm sick.

Maj. Be gad, you needn't be afraid, look at "old never fail."

Ebony. Say, boss, we want to all stay together.

Maj. Of course we do, you and me and "old never fail." Gad, boy, we will show 'em. I'll get the gin and peppermint.

Ebony. Say, boss, is there goin' to be any knockin's down in this?

Maj. Be gad, sah, I'm Major Dolittle, from Kentucky—

Ebony. Say, I golly, we want to all stay together now?

Maj. Why, of course we do! You run on down the street and I'll go and get the gin and peppermint, and then we will go.

Ebony. (*start* R.) We'll show 'em I golly; (*turns*) we want to all stay together boss, all stay together. (*exit*, R.

Maj. Yes, we'll all stay together; come out here "old never fail."

(*flourishes revolver*

Enter, MACK, L. E.

Mack. Hello! there Major, how goes the battle?

Maj. Say, Landlord, be gad, sah, do you know a fellow by the name of Guy Lester?

Mack. Can't say that I do. Why?

Maj. Be gad, sah, I'd like to see him; he's a runaway nigger—used to be one of my slaves before the war. He and his sister ran away from me; curse 'em. They've got my brand on their hands Be gad, sah, if I find him, me and "old never fail" proposes to anihilate him, sah, we'll blow a hole through his diabolical heart that you can throw a chinese bible through. We are looking for blood—me and "old never rail", and be gad, sah, I'll go and get some gin and peppermint. (*exit*, R.

Mack. Thunder! luck's coming my way at last, that's what I call information worth something. I always thought Lester had a secret, and at last I've found it out. He called me slave driver—nigger whipper, and now then I'll be even with him—I'll call him "slave-runaway nigger," I'll throw that in his face, curse him. (*exit*, R.

SCENE II.—Cave in the Mountain.

GUY R. *Enter,* JENNIE, L. E.

Jen.. (*runs to* GUY) O! Guy! Guy!

Guy. What is the matter, Jennie, tell me quick, what have you seen or heard?

Jen. We will have to leave—Major Dolittle is here—in Toomstone.

Guy. Well, what of that, he don't know us.

Jen. O! he does—he does, he stopped me on the street, recognized me, called me a slave—a runaway nigger. O! Guy, I could hardly keep from killing him. He said he would soon pay you a visit and settle accounts with you—

Guy. Let him, curse him, he will never pay another man a visit. When he hunts Guy Lester, he will have hunted up his last man. We both wear his mark and curse him, he shall wear mine—Jennie, you are excited, go in and bring Nell to this room. See that she does not escape—I must go and see if Mack is coming.

Jen. Are we always to hear the words "slave-runaway niggers?"
(*exit,* R.

Guy. No! by heavens we'll not, I'll not be hounded down by him, curse him. (*exit,* L.

Enter, JENNIE *and* NELL, *from* R. E,, NELL *bound by chain*—JENNIE *fastens chain to rock.*

Jen. You're a beauty, you are, and you've got yourself in a nice fix too, haven't you? Maybe you will learn to let other people's business alone after this—see what you've got yourself into by your meddling. O! you are a *sweet one.*

Nell. If these chains were off of me and I had my rifle, you wouldn't talk that way to me, I'd put a hole through that treacherous heart of yours.

Jen. Yes "if!" Why don't you break the chains. Don't tell me I'm treacherous, you are the one that will have to be watched, you are the one that is treacherous. Who started the Regulators after us? Why you did.

Nell. No I didn't either, but if I ever get out of this I will, you can bet your dust on that.

Jen. Well, I'll take good care that you never get out alive.

Nell. Ah! you wouldn't kill anybody, you haven't got the courage—it takes courage to kill people—you and that sneaking brother of yours—both together—haven't the courage of a rag doll.

Jen. Shut up, don't provoke me too far or I'll—I'll—(*draws dirk*) I'll cut that throat of yours.

Nell. Ah! go away, you tire me—run down to your play-house, sissy, and play with your dolls.

Jen. You'll never say that again.
(*raises dirk and advances about to strike*

Enter, MACK, R., 2 E.

Mack. Hold on there, what the thunder are you trying to do? Drop that knife.

Jen. I'll kill her!

Mack. No! you won't either, I've got something to say about that, put up that "sticker."

Nell. Let that coward alone, she won't hurt anybody.

Mack. Shut up Nell, this has gone far enough. Where is Guy, Jennie?

Jen. I don't know, hunt him up if you want him.

Mack. I will, and I'll surprise him when I do find him, too. I've a little account to settle with him and you too. You've called me slave-driver and nigger whipper long enough, now then I'll get even with you both. I've found you out—I know you—you are octoroons—slaves—runaway niggers—you have the slave brand on your hands.

JENNIE *raises dager and rushes upon* MACK, *strikes him, he staggers back, she strikes again, he falls* C., *she strikes again.*

Enter, GUY, L. E.

Guy. Jennie! Jennie! heavens girl, what have you done?

Jen. O! Guy, I've killed him—he called us slaves, runaway niggers—

Guy. We have no time for explanations, the Regulators are after us—almost upon us. This country is too warm for us, we must leave. Come! hurry! they are just coming down the mountain; hurry girl or we will be taken.

Nell. Cowards! cowards! I'll shoot both of you yet.

JENNIE *runs back to* NELL, *raises dirk to strike,* GUY *jerks her out* R.

Ebony. (*out* L.) Now boss, we want to all stay together.

Maj. (*out* L.) Come out here "old never fail," where's the gin and peppermint? Here it is, now be gad, let's go. (*calls*) Don't shoot, don't shoot, we're friends, we're friends, etc.

Enter, EBONY *and* MAJOR, L. E., MAJOR *pushing* EBONY *in, trying to hide behind him.*

Ebony. I golly, boss, let's all stay together.

Maj. Don't shoot, don't shoot, be gad. I'll take some gin and pepperment. (*sees* MACK *on stage, points revolver over* EBONY's *shoulder*) Throw up your hands, be gad, sah, "old never fail" has got the drop on you.

Nell. (*calls*) Ebony!

Ebony. I golly, Miss Nell, dat you? (*runs to her*)

Maj. (*goes to* NELL) Well, be gad, sah, you're pretty well tied up, ain't you? Here, take some gin and peppermint, and I'll soon get you loose. (*unlocks chains,* NELL *rises*)

Maj. (*goes to* MACK) Now then, be gad, if you are dead, say so, and if you ain't, why take some gin and peppermint. (*kneels over* MACK

Ebony. I golly, Miss Nell, I done thought that you'se clear outen sight, now I done told yer I did.

Nell. So did I, Ebony.

Mack. (*calls*) Nell!

Maj. Be gad, landlord, you ain't dead yet, are you? Here, take some more gin and peppermint. (*business*

Mack. Nell! come here. (NELL *goes* C.) Don't hold anything against me, Nell, will you?

Nell. Well Mack, you've treated me badly—

Mack. I know I have, Nell, but you'll forgive me, won't you? I am dying Nell, and I want to tell you something. Listen, Nell, my name is Fred Eldair; my oldest brother Joe, left Boston and came to the West—to Toombstone—you knew him as Sacramento Joe. I didn't know he was my brother until I had killed him— (*stops*

Maj. Here, take some more of the gin and peppermint.

(business

Mack. While I was in Boston, I was cashier in Arthur Brandon's bank—he detected me in stealing from him, but as I was young, he left me go free, and in return for his kindness toward me, I stole his child. The child was named Gracie; she was then about two years old—I fled to the South with her, and then West—well, you know the rest, Nell—all but this—the child I stole from Arthur Brandon was you, Nell—Arthur Brandon is your father.

(sinks back on stage

Ebony. I golly, if dat don't beat the debil!

Maj. Well, be gad, I should say so, and the gin and peppermint is all gone, let's go to Toomstone and get some more.

Nell. But, can we take him with us?

Maj. I'm Major Dolittle, from Kentucky, sah, and be gad, I'll try. (*they raise* MACK *up)* I sign my name with an X, and be gad, we will get some more gin and peppermint. *(exeunt, L.*

*SCENE III.—*MACK's *saloon.*

Enter, MAJOR *and* NELL, L., 3 E., BELL, R. E.

Bell. O! Nell! Nell! I am so glad to have you back again!

Maj. (*behind bar)* Gad, if I could find that gin and peppermint.

Nell. I told you I'd soon be back, Bell.

Bell. And Jerry? Have you seen anything of him?

Nell. Try not to think about that Bell, he is—he will never come back—

Bell. Is he—he is not—not—

Nell. Yes, Bell, he is dead; we tried to bring him down the mountain, but he died before we got half way.

Maj. Yes, the gin and peppermint give out. If that had held out, we'd got him here all right. (BELL *weeps*

Nell. Don't grieve about it Bell, it's better that he should be dead. He was a murderer, for he killed old Joe, and Joe was his brother. He told me the history of his life before he died—he told me that Arthur Brandon was my father, and he has all of the proofs, we just came from my father's house; and Bell, we are to leave Toomstone to-morrow forever, and you are going with us.

Bell. O! Nell, you are too good and kind, I can not express my thanks in words, I—I—I—I don't know what to do.

Maj. Come up and take some gin and peppermint with me.

Enter, CHARLEY, L. E.

Chas. Ah! Nell, back in the "Gold Dust" again, alive and well I see—Ah! good-morning, Bell.

Nell. Yes, Charley, back again—how did the dust and the papers turn out, all right?

Chas. Yes, all right, the dust was all there, just to the ounce, and the papers for "Claim 96" were all right too. I heard you were going to leave in the morning, so I came around to try to thank you for the good turn you done me by returning the dust and papers.

Nell. Don't thank me, thank the Major; if it hadn't been for him, I would still be a prisoner on the mountain.

Chas. Well, Major—

Maj. Be gad, sah, you needn't thank me, "old never fail" is the one that done the work. I'm Major Dolittle, from Kentucky, sah, come up and take some gin and peppermint with me and "old never fail."

Nell. I don't suppose that we could persuade you to go back to the East with us, Charley?

Chas. No! Nell, I expect to leave the West some time, but not now. I have too much at stake to leave now. I shall work "Claim 96" for all she is worth—I may go to the East in a year, or may be sooner, but not now—and you Bell, I suppose that you—

Bell. Yes, I'm to go with Nell. She says I must, and I suppose I shall have too. She has been my best friend, and I have tried to be a friend to her—

Nell. And you have succeeded too, Bell.

Chas. And you Major, I suppose you are going to—

Maj. I'm going to 'tend bar in the "Gold Dust" be gad, sah. Come up and have some gin and peppermint.

Chas. Well, it seems as if everything is all ready for you to make an early start in the morning—

Enter, EBONY, L. E.

Ebony. Well, hold on, I golly, here's me yet—if you'se all goin' away, what's goin' to come o' me? What am I goin' to do? Are you done goin' to leave me back here to be hoo-dooed? What you goin' to do with dis chile?

Maj. Give him some gin and peppermint, be gad, sah.

Nell. What do you want us to do with you, Ebony?

Ebony. I golly, I don't know Miss Nell, does you?

Nell. Do you want to go with us?

Ebony. I golly, can I?

Nell. Yes, if you want too.

Ebony. Whoop! (*yells*) dis chile's done outen sight now, I done tole yer.

Maj. And so am I and "old never fail," and be gad, sah, we'll take some gin and peppermint.   (*drinks*

Nell. Ebony, you've done me several good turns, and if you was'nt so much on the brunette order, I'd kiss you.

Maj. (*comes from behind bar, bottle in hand*) Well, be gad, sah, here's one a shade lighter—I'm Major Dolittle, from Kentucky, sah; used to own one hundred niggers. I sign my name with an X, and be gad, sah, I'll take some gin and peppermint.   (*drinks*

MAJOR C.   NELL L. C.

CHARLEY R.   EBONY R. C.   BELL L.

CURTAIN.

THE END.

www.ingramcontent.com/pod-product-compliance
Lightning Source LLC
Chambersburg PA
CBHW022206020726
47496CB00008B/2899